I0645345

Zax and the Three Beasts

Dennis Eaves

Copyright © Dennis Eaves 2021

Written by Dennis Eaves
Cover Design by Dennis Eaves
Edited by Stacy Matkins
Book Design by Cliff Matkins

This book is a work of fiction. Names, characters, places, and incidents either are products of the author's imagination or are used fictitiously. Any resemblance to actual events or locales or persons, living or dead, is entirely coincidental.

All rights reserved. No portion of this book may be reproduced in any form by any electronic or mechanical means including information and storage systems—except in the case of brief quotations embodied in critical articles or reviews—without permission in writing from:

Lea Street Press, LLC
Blanch, NC
Leastreetpress.com
Leastreetpress@gmail.com

Issued in print and in electronic formats.

ISBN 978-0-9998717-6-8 (softcover)
ISBN 978-0-9998717-7-5 (ebook)

Library of Congress Control Number: 2021900199

This book is dedicated to all those who inspired, encouraged, and believed in me. Special thanks to my high school english teacher. Ms. Jessen, to Lea Street Press, LLC and to my family.

It's been quite a ride!

Zax and the Three Beasts

Prologue

Ok, let's say there is a large, bright, unknown sphere of pure energy buried deep inside the core of the earth that is attracted to one thing—and only one thing. That *thing* is a shy, blonde, blue-eyed, six-foot tall teenage boy named Zax. And Zax has no idea that the energy is attracted to him.

The Beginning

1

Zax stared out his bedroom window at the unusual sight of sunshine and wondered how long it would be before the next rain came. But living on the outskirts of a small, rural town about thirty miles southwest of Tacoma, Washington, he already knew the answer—not long.

He pulled the covers over his head and wished he had another half-hour to sleep before having to get ready for another agonizing day at school. The source of his agony was clear. His parents refused to allow him to have or be around any high-tech electronic devices. Not having a cell phone or being able to use a computer at school was pure torture. From a teenager's perspective, it was worse than having the plague.

Most kids at school bullied him or called him "Caveman"; others simply ignored him. And all because, to them, he was "not up to date." To make matters even worse, his parents had gone to the school board and, citing their "religious beliefs," had gotten approval to keep him out of all classes that required the use of any high-tech devices. He'd really hoped that this year, his junior year, they would have changed their minds. It didn't happen. And they wondered why he didn't have friends.

The only reason his parents had ever given for their decision was that it was for his own good. He didn't understand—and was told he didn't need to—but doubted that was the case. Since they were not particularly religious and considering there was not one single high-tech device in their home, he thought it might be that they simply couldn't afford the cost and didn't want to admit it. It seemed like a logical conclusion to draw since they lived a simple lifestyle in a small white house, next to a lake, with no neighbors nearby. They didn't travel or socialize very much with people from town, but occasionally, they did go see a movie or eat at one of the many chain restaurants in Tacoma. These outings were one of the few things that Zax enjoyed in his life.

Zax walked through the living room to the kitchen, and the weatherman on their vintage television—which broadcast only local channels via an antenna on the roof—confirmed his prediction of rain.

That was his life—teen of the stone age. Then a new kid moved into town, and everything changed.

2

Zax rounded the corner and entered his english classroom thinking it was going to be just another typical day. English had never been his favorite subject, but Ms. Jessen had a teaching style that made english fascinating. Her class was quickly moving up the ladder.

As Zax was settling down in his seat, something caught his eye. A new kid was standing in front of the classroom. Not just any kid. A girl. A girl with long blonde hair, about 5'7" with brown eyes. She had on a black t-shirt, a denim jacket, jeans, and black and white Vans.

"Class," Ms. Jessen announced, "this is Jaiden Maynard." She opened her hand and fanned her arm around the classroom while looking for an open seat. "Jaiden, this is our class. It looks like there is an empty seat next to Zax. Zax, raise your hand, please."

Zax could not believe his luck. The only seat available was next to him. He instantly thought that this was going to be a good day—or at least better than most.

Zax still could not believe his luck as Jaiden walked to her desk. In a class where seventy-five percent of the students were boys and about twenty-five percent of those were football players, having a new girl was definitely a nice change of pace.

Zax shuffled in his seat. He thought he would try and quickly make friends with her before anyone introduced him as "Caveman." He'd hoped for a long time that he would have at least one friend—even if for only a short time—while he was still in high school. *Maybe she's the one,* he thought as Jaiden sat down next to him.

"Hey," he whispered, "I'm Zax."

"Nice to meet you," Jaiden replied while putting her phone away.

"You too. Did you move here or what?"

"Yeah, I moved from Indiana."

"Cool. So why did you move here?" Zax asked. *Really, Zax?* he thought. *That's your best attempt at conversation? No wonder you don't have friends.*

"Oh um, my parents found jobs outside of Tacoma, and I had to come with them," she said, fumbling to get situated.

"Lucky us," Zax mumbled. Smiling, he opened his textbook to Chapter 10.

3

So now things in the english class went back to being normal. This included things like putting up with Jack Jason, the bully who sat on the other side of him. Jack had short brown hair, was 6'2", weighed about 250—all muscle—and had hazel eyes. He was the quarterback for the high school football team, and he was an idiot unless he really studied. Then he was only average.

Every day after the bell rang to start class, he would say, "Hey, Caveman. Did you watch…oh wait, I forgot you don't have technology in the rock ages." It always amazed Zax that Jack couldn't come up with something new to torment him, but it confirmed his opinion that Jack was, in fact, an idiot. And an idiot with a limited vocabulary.

"Hey, Caveman. Did you watch…oh wait, I forgot you don't have technology in the rock ages," Jack said, a little louder than most days to make sure Jaiden heard.

Zax ignored him; he always did. But Jaiden did not.

"Hey, new girl, you know I'm the quarterback. It's unfortunate you got stuck with Caveman here, and not the jock of the school," Jack said, then laughed.

"You know, I didn't know what quarterback meant before, but in your case, I think it means you have a quarter of a brain. And it's the 'stone ages,' not the 'rock ages,' genius," she snapped. She turned her head back to her desk.

Who is this girl? Zax thought, surprised.

Jack looked at her in shock. No one had ever shown him up. No one had ever tried. For whatever reason, everyone seemed afraid of him. But apparently, Jaiden was not everyone. Zax knew a retaliation was coming once the dunce realized that she had totally hammered him.

Jack angrily jumped out of his seat and marched over to Jaiden with his fist raised. When Zax saw what was about to happen, he sprung from his desk and, with an astonishing burst of strength, grabbed Jack's arm and threw him across the room. It was like a reflex, just something that happened without thinking.

Instantly, Zax saw flickers of yellow specks. He thought they were from his adrenalin, but as they lingered, he suddenly began fearing his own strength. A few months ago, he could barely lift fifty pounds, let alone a football quarterback. Everyone looked at him with astonishment, but they weren't the only ones afraid.

Jack gripped his right arm, and from the pained look on his face, Zax knew he was hurt.

Everyone in the class was taking videos with their phones or calling the nurse's office.

Zax turned pale. *What did I just do?*

The next thing Zax knew, he was sent to the principal's office, note in hand.

4

Principal Hart was about 5'8" with short black hair, green eyes, and was clueless about half the things that happened in the school. He was pretty laid back most of the time, but when it came to football, he was all over it. No one really knew why; he just was. Zax's theory was that he used to play football but was never good enough to play for a big-time team. But that's all it was, a theory.

Zax got to the principal's office and stood outside the doorway. Principal Hart was intently reading a document and didn't notice he was there until Zax made himself cough.

Principal Hart peered over his reading glasses. "Oh, Zax, I didn't see you. Come in and have a seat," he said as he laid his glasses on his desk. "What can I do for you?" he asked attentively.

Clearly, he doesn't know what I just did to Jack, Zax thought. *Based on his demeanor, he must think I'm here to talk about social problems or something.*

Zax handed Principal Hart the hall pass that Ms. Jessen had given him. Principal Hart stared at it for a moment, then calmly picked up his phone and called the nurse's office.

"I see," Principal Hart said.   Zax could see Principal Hart's face changing before his eyes. "Keep me posted on Jack's condition."

With that, the phone call ended. Principal Hart slammed the phone down and bolted out of his chair.

Here we go, Zax thought, bracing himself.

"Why would you do that? The big game is coming up, and you've injured our best player!" he barked as he stormed out of his office. "Stay where you are!"

When Principal Hart returned about half an hour later, Zax tried explaining to him that Jack was about to punch the new girl, but he didn't care. All he cared about was their stupid football season and getting to the playoffs. After what seemed like an eternity of lectures on how important football was to the school, Principal Hart finally got around to Zax's punishment. His sentence: lunchtime detention for two weeks.

Zax accepted his punishment without saying a word, then stood and walked out the door.

5

The lunch bell rang just as Zax was leaving the principal's office, so he bypassed his locker and went straight to the lunchroom. He grabbed a chicken sandwich, fries, and a Dr. Pepper, then took his lunch and sat down at his usual spot in the corner, alone, all while being taunted by kids waving their phones in his face.

"Hey, did you get the new iPhone?" one kid smirked. "Oh wait, you don't even have a flip phone. That's right," he laughed and walked away with his group of friends. That was lunch. Every day. Monday through Friday.

Zax unscrewed the lid of his drink and looked up to see Jaiden heading his way. *Oh, great!* he thought. *She must have seen what just happened.*

"Mind if I join you?" she asked.

"Not sure why you'd want to," Zax said under his breath.

"You stopped Jack from punching me. I owe you this much at least," she said. She looked at his lunch and realized it was identical to hers. "And we both like chicken sandwiches."

They both chuckled. In this moment, Zax felt like his wish for a friend might actually come true.

"Hey, do you want to listen to some music with me?" she asked, pulling earbuds from her jacket pocket. "I'll take one, and you take the other. I'll even let you pick the songs."

This wasn't the first time someone had offered to let Zax listen to music using their earbuds. One time, a guy named Steve, who Zax thought was a fellow outcast, had offered. But when Zax tried to take them, Steve yanked them away and laughed. *Guess I was wrong about who he was,* Zax remembered thinking.

Zax didn't say anything. He put his head down and took another bite of his sandwich. He held it with both hands so he didn't have to explain why he couldn't take the earbuds.

The next thing he knew, rock music was blasting into his left ear. He jumped, startled by the sudden noise. Jaiden had placed an earbud in his ear. She had no way of knowing that Zax was not supposed to come in contact with high-tech devices.

She giggled and tried handing her phone to Zax to make up for scaring him. He hesitated, trying to decide what to do. He really wanted her to become his friend. And, because of that, he felt like he had no choice but to take it. He was afraid if he didn't take the phone, she would freak out and decide to get up and leave—ruining any chance of them becoming friends. Besides, he had never held a phone and really wanted to.

He held out his hand, knowing that he probably shouldn't, and he was right. Once Jaiden's phone hit his hand, he saw a weird stream of energy jump from his hand to the phone. *My eyes must be playing tricks on me. Didn't get a lot of sleep last night,* he thought. *Oh, well.*

Jaiden took the earbud out of her ear and handed it to Zax. He put it in his other ear but heard nothing. He instantly felt different. He felt energized. It was as if he had a completely new body. Like something had entered his veins, something powerful. But again, he thought it was just because he didn't get enough sleep, so he shrugged it off.

"Should I hear music from this one too?" he asked, removing the earbud she'd just handed him.

"You don't?" she asked, extending her hand. "It was literally working one second ago."

Zax handed the phone back to her, but she dropped it as soon as it touched her hand.

"It's burning hot!" she shouted.

Zax saw radiating streams of bright energy coming off the phone. But the energy looked oddly familiar, like something he'd seen all his life. He grabbed the phone off the floor—where scorch marks had formed in the shape of the phone—and chunked it through an open window. For some reason, like earlier with Jack, it was just a reflex. The phone did not seem hot to him, nor did it burn his fingers. He and Jaiden rushed to the window and stared down at the phone. It was still glowing hot and had started emitting an unusual light. Once the light went away, it looked normal again. But a mark was left on the ground where it landed; the same kind of mark left on the lunch room floor where Jaiden had dropped it.

Jaiden looked at Zax in disbelief. "What did you do?" she asked with a shaky voice.

"Nothing," Zax shrugged. "You know how phones have been blowing up these days," he said nervously, not knowing what else to say.

"I guess, yeah," she said with an uncertain smile.

Zax knew that wasn't the case, though, and he was determined to find out what was going on once he got home.

Secrets

6

After school, Zax headed home with one question on his mind; *what is happening to me?* He looked down his long, narrow, pine tree-lined driveway at the white two-story, perfectly square house he called home. He knew he was responsible for Jaiden's phone in some way. He couldn't shake the familiarity he felt with the energy.

As soon as he got home, he told his parents everything that had happened. Jenny Klein, his mom, was 5'7" with a medium build, long brown hair and a sweet smile. Ethan Klein, his dad, was about six feet tall with a somewhat stocky build and short black hair. He had a very demanding, abrasive personality that in recent years had driven a wedge between him and Zax.

As Zax talked, his parents looked at each other with apprehension in their eyes, then back at him with that same concern.

"What were you doing with a phone?" Ethan demanded.

Zax stared at them. *I'm fine, thanks for asking. Not like I could've gotten hurt from this,* he thought. He wondered if his dad could hear his thoughts. He hoped so.

"I was only holding it. The phone was emitting a weird energy, and then it became hot enough to mark the concrete. That's all. Nothing bad or anything. A new friend let me use it because I was alone at lunch, as usual."

A slight grin came on Jenny's face and, for a moment, it seemed as though she'd forgotten about the phone. "A new friend? Could this new friend be a girl?"

"It's nothing like that, ok!" Zax said, clearly annoyed.

Ethan, on the other hand, had a furious scowl on his face, as always. "What did we tell you about high-tech devices?" he yelled.

"That it would be for my own good if I don't use one," Zax said. "But you didn't give any logical reason. You just said—without any explanation—that I'm not allowed to use anything high-tech. That's it. Nothing else, just that."

"I shouldn't have to tell you anything else. You *should* have followed my instructions. You're just a kid. You don't need to know everything," Ethan said, still yelling.

Zax could feel himself getting angry. "Don't play the 'you're just a kid' card on me. I'm not an idiot!"

"Go to your room!" Ethan yelled.

"Not like I can do anything else in this stupid house that's in the middle of nowhere," Zax said as he turned and walked off, leaving Jenny and Ethan standing in the living room. He didn't call Jenny "mom" or Ethan "dad" because—for some reason—he didn't see them as his parents. He didn't know why, but he'd never gotten that parent feeling from them. Never.

Zax still had the strange sensation he felt earlier, like something new was running through his veins. He tried to ignore it, but it was hard to shake off what happened with the phone. He remembered that when the phone got red hot, he saw visions of monsters. It was as if they were his memories, but the last time he checked, he'd never seen any monsters, not even in the movies. He was sure it was just a dream.

Zax heard Jenny and Ethan talking downstairs, so he decided to do what every teenager who gets in trouble does—he started to eavesdrop.

"This is bad," Ethan said. Even though Zax couldn't see him, he envisioned Ethan running his hand through his hair. Ethan always did this when he was nervous.

"Maybe the energy has secluded by now," Jenny said.

"It doesn't matter. It doesn't just seclude. If it's used in any way, then it stays for good."

"The organization will not be happy with this," Jenny sighed.

Now, Zax had even more questions. *What energy? What organization?* He sat quietly and didn't know if he would ever have answers. What he *did* know, however, was that if Jenny and Ethan caught him listening to their conversation, they would be furious—even more so than when they sent him to his room. Past experience told him that. He knew he had to get back to his bedroom before he was spotted.

Zax slipped back into his room and flopped on his bed. He usually stayed there all weekend—every weekend—since he couldn't really do anything else. High-tech electronic devices were everywhere, and Jenny and Ethan were determined to keep them away from him. But right now, he wanted more. He wanted to hear music again, he wanted to feel the weight of a phone in his hand again, or maybe, he thought, it was that he just wanted to see Jaiden again.

7

Zax looked out his window and saw the tall pine trees swaying. Without a second thought, he decided to do something he had never considered before. He decided to sneak out of his window and climb down the trellis. He lifted the unscreened window and stepped over the sill.

All was going well until he got about halfway down. His hand slipped, and he started to fall backwards. His mind flooded with thoughts of never going back to school if Ethan and Jenny found him lying in the patchy grass with both legs broken. But that was simply wishful thinking.

Once he started falling, Zax stretched his arms out as far as he possibly could and tried to grab hold of the trellis. He felt as though he were floating in slow motion. His arms felt warm and tingly. He was determined to catch the trellis, but he closed his eyes just in case. He didn't want to see the ground racing towards him. By some miracle, he was able to grab the wooden latticework and pull himself back up.

After he caught his breath, he noticed yellow flecks again. The flecks were the same as the ones he'd seen when he threw Jack across the room. He assumed they, too, were caused by adrenaline.

Zax carefully resumed his downward trek and descended to the ground without any problem. With his feet firmly underneath him, he bent over and kissed the ground. He'd never been so happy to be standing on a patch of dirt.

8

Zax walked into town and hoped to find something to do that would keep him out of trouble. He had caused enough havoc for one day. When he got to Town Park, he strolled over to the farthest bench and sat down. His mind was still running wild trying to figure out what Ethan and Jenny meant when they said "organization" and "energy," if the two were connected, and if so, how. The next thing he knew, someone popped him in the back of the head.

"Ow! What do you think…" Zax said as he turned around and saw Jaiden. "Oh, what are you doing here?" he asked.

"Getting payback for what you did to my phone. It was destroyed, and everything was erased! All that was on the screen were yellow swirls."

"Yellow swirls?" he asked curiously.

"Yeah, it looked like some kind of crazy energy flow. It was really weird."

"Energy?" he mumbled to himself.

"What are you whispering about? You know, you're going to have to pay me back for destroying my phone."

"But I don't have any money," he said, embarrassed.

"Who said anything about money? I have something else in mind," she smirked. "Come on," she said and motioned for him to follow.

They walked a couple of blocks to her house. The two-story brick house had a covered front porch that ran the entire length of the house. It had a wicker swing hanging from the ceiling on one end, and two rocking chairs sat on the opposite end. But the best part of the house was that Jaiden had neighbors on both sides. *Wish we lived in town,* Zax thought, waving at her neighbor.

Jaiden unlocked the door, and Zax quickly realized her parents weren't home.

"Where are your parents?" he asked as he sat down on the couch in the living room.

"They're at work," she replied.

"So, how do you want me to pay you back?" he asked, hoping she could not detect his anxiety.

She sat down next to him and stared into his eyes.

"You have pretty eyes," she said.

"Um, ok? I mean, thank you," he said awkwardly. Not knowing what else to say, he nervously added, "So, what do you want me to do?"

She leaned back, slouching on the couch.

"Make me a three-course meal," she announced.

"Wait, so you want me to become your chef?" he chuckled.

"Yup, pretty much."

"But I've never cooked before."

"What! How have you never cooked before?" she asked, bolting back upright on the couch.

"I've never needed to. Jenny is an excellent cook," he said and paused for a second. "Ethan, on the other hand, well, he can't even boil water."

"Fine. I'll give you until Sunday at 2:00 to learn how to cook me a delicious three-course-meal," she said.

"2:00? This Sunday?" he said panicked. "Why does cooking have to be how I repay you? And why so soon?"

"Because that's what I want. You can learn how to cook, and we can get to know each other better. Besides, my parents have a church event that afternoon," she said. "But I'm gonna be watching you. I don't want you burning down my house," she laughed.

"Ok, if you say so," he shrugged.

9

Zax left Jaiden's house a short time later. Once he got home, he climbed back up the trellis and through his window. He went downstairs to find Jenny sitting in the living room by herself.

"Where's Ethan?"

"He was called into work. An emergency came up at the factory," Jenny replied.

For as long as Zax could remember, he'd been told that Ethan worked for the phone manufacturer, P. Inc. The story was that Ethan started out as a low-level apprentice and, over the years, had worked his way up to become a supervisor. He was a technical wizard, and P. Inc. knew it; thus, he was their "go-to" guy when a crisis arose.

Despite Ethan's lack of a formal education, he'd done well. He managed to provide his family with a comfortable, albeit simple life that allowed Jenny to stay home and take care of all the household stuff like money, taxes, bills, and, most importantly, groceries. At least that's how it appeared to Zax.

"Ok. Hey, um, I was wondering if you could teach me how to cook?" Zax asked, staring at the ridiculous cat picture hanging by the front door. He didn't know why Ethan liked cats so much. It was odd, especially since they didn't have one and never had.

"I didn't know you were interested in cooking," Jenny said as she removed her reading glasses and looked up from her crossword puzzle.

"Well, I was thinking that if you were gone and Ethan had to cook and—so I don't get food poisoning—then I probably should learn to cook," he managed to say.

"It could be that..." she smiled. "Or, more likely, it could have something to do with you sneaking out of the house."

"I, I don't know what you're talking about," he stammered.

"You know, unlike Ethan, I don't care if you go into town. You could've used the front door."

"Yes, but Ethan was here when I left. I snuck out and went to the park. I ran into the person whose phone I destroyed, and they want me to pay them back by making a delicious three-course-meal," he said quickly, hoping Jenny wouldn't ask any more questions.

"You know, by not saying 'him' or 'her', you're just confirming that this person is a girl," she teased.

Zax smiled shyly and looked at the floor. "It is a girl. Her name is Jaiden."

"That's a pretty name. Tell me..."

"Yeah, so about the cooking thing?" he interrupted, trying to get out of this conversation.

"Of course I'll teach you! I'll show you how to become a culinary god!" she said, standing up dramatically. "Come on. It'll be fun."

Jenny started with the basics, like how to keep the kitchen clean and stirring techniques. After a two-hour lesson, Zax was in kitchen overload and asked Jenny if they could continue the next morning. She was more than willing since that meant spending time with him on a Saturday. The only interaction she usually had with him on the weekends was when she knocked on his door and asked if he was ok or needed anything.

10

Zax glanced at his alarm clock as the sun peered in through his bedroom window. It was seven-thirty, and for once, he was unopposed to getting out of bed this early, particularly on a Saturday. He rushed down to the kitchen, ready for his cooking lesson, where Jenny had pancakes and bacon waiting. Within half an hour, they had eaten, cleaned the kitchen, and were ready to start Lesson Two—baking cakes and sweets. After that, they were off to soups and how to cut vegetables and meat correctly. By late afternoon, he was quite sure he had learned more about cooking, in one day, than he had learned about anything else in his entire life, which wasn't saying much.

11

When it came time to go to Jaiden's the next afternoon, Zax asked Jenny to drive him rather than relying on his own two feet to get him there. He wanted to be on his game in the kitchen when he arrived and wanted to impress Jaiden with his newly acquired skills. Besides, they had to stop by the local market to get the groceries, and toting bags of groceries down the street would only further his uncoolness.

After grabbing the stuff on his list at the grocery store and putting it in the car, they were off to Jaiden's. As the car slowed for the approaching intersection at Main Street and Third Avenue, Zax saw an energy in the form of yellow swirls begin to emit from the traffic light. He looked at Jenny and wondered if she saw them or if it was just him. She continued talking, and it was clear she did not. Zax turned his attention back to the swirls and thought about what she and Ethan said about the energy. He couldn't help but think these swirls must have had something to do with it.

"Is something wrong?" Jenny asked at his abrupt silence. Until he saw the swirls, they had been talking nonstop.

"No, just thinking," he replied, not wanting to alarm her—or himself for that matter.

"Like?" she asked.

"Just life," he said as he turned and stared out the passenger's window.

"Your meal is going to be perfect," she encouraged. "You've got nothing to worry about."

It's not the meal I'm worried about, he thought.

12

When they got to Jaiden's, Zax grabbed the groceries out of the back seat and told Jenny he would call her later to come pick him up. As he stepped onto the porch, he turned around and noticed Jenny was still in the driveway. About that time, Jaiden flung open the front door.

Seeing the car, she stepped out and waved. "Is that your Mom?"

"Yeah," he said. "I don't have a car, either." *No phone, no car...she has to think I'm a freak*, he thought.

Once they got inside, Zax peered out the window to make sure Jenny had left. It was more than obvious, he thought, that she'd waited to leave until she saw what Jaiden looked like.

"Are you ready to pay up?" Jaiden giggled.

"I think so," Zax smiled. He stepped out of the foyer into the living room with two plastic bags draped over each arm.

"Good," she said, "because I'm hungry. Need some help with the bags?"

"I got it," he said, trying hard to erase the swirls of energy from his mind.

"Ok. Follow me, and I'll show you the kitchen."

Jaiden walked ahead of him, and with every step she took, the swirls seemed to fade.

Zax sat the groceries down on the dining bar that separated the kitchen from the living room. Two aprons were neatly folded near the sink, and a fire extinguisher was sitting in the middle of the stovetop. He grinned and pointed at the fire extinguisher. "Don't you trust me?"

"It's good to take precautions," she joked as she picked it up and pointed it at him.

"Well, you won't need it," he said with a smug face. "I am now a culinary god!"

Jaiden laughed. "Well, show me, so-called 'culinary god,' what you can do," she said, waving her hands across the kitchen. They both laughed as he put on the blue apron that read "Chef in the House."

Zax started by making sure he had a clean workplace and that everything he needed—including utensils and ingredients—was close by. According to Jenny, this was the absolute first step. He took the items from the bags and organized them on the bar. It was time to get busy.

After much debate the night before, he had decided to make french fries for the appetizer. The good ones, though, the ones with lots of seasoning on them.

Zax peeled five potatoes, then, using a french fry cutter, he sliced them into perfect shape. Sticking potatoes in a cutter and pushing down a handle was definitely the best way to cut his gourmet fries. Once he had a full plate, he tossed some seasoning on them and dropped them in a skillet of hot oil. A few minutes later, his first course was complete. He sprinkled a little more seasoning on the hot fries and set the plate in front of Jaiden.

"Hmmm…they look good and smell good, but the main question is," she paused, "do they taste good?" Jaiden grabbed one and put it in her mouth. Her eyes widened so big that Zax swore he literally saw them sparkle.

"So, how are they?" he asked, crossing his fingers behind his back.

She swallowed and closed her eyes. *She must have known they were sparkling, too*, he thought.

"They are acceptable," she said as she wiped her mouth with a napkin.

Acceptable? he thought. He grabbed one and tasted for himself. *She must be kidding. These are REALLY good!* He'd followed Jenny's instructions explicitly, and these fries were pure perfection.

As she was munching on his "acceptable" fries, he started course two—hamburgers. Burgers were one of the only things to go well with french fries, so it seemed like a logical choice. When the patties were seasoned and shaped, Zax took them outside and neatly positioned them on the hot backyard grill. While they were grilling, he went back inside to cut up the lettuce and tomatoes.

"So, how did you end up in this small town?" Jaiden asked.

Zax pondered the question for a moment. He'd never thought much about the size of their town until she said, "small town." Oddly, it suddenly occurred to him that they did, in fact, live in a small town. There was only one subdivision, one grocery store, two red lights, and a burger joint called Harvey's. Rumors had floated around town for years that Dollar General and McDonald's might be coming, but Zax had long given up hope on getting a Big Mac every day.

"I've been here my whole life. Or at least as far back as I can remember," he said, praying he wouldn't cut himself while slicing the tomatoes.

"What do you mean?"

"Well, I can only remember back to when I was twelve. I don't have any memories before then."

"Wait. What? How is that even possible?" she asked curiously. "You don't remember anything before age 12?"

"I don't know how it's possible, but I have a theory. I'm not sure, though," he said, grabbing the condiments out of the fridge.

"Well...what is it? What's your theory?" she asked eagerly.

"Sometimes I have dreams of things I've never seen before," he said.

"Like what?" She leaned forward in her barstool and put her elbows on the bar, resting her head in her hands.

"Like giant canyons and oceans with water so clear that you can see forever beneath your feet. As far as I know or can remember, I've never been to a place like that. My theory is that I had amnesia from an accident and that Ethan and Jenny wanted me to be different than how I use to be. Be right back," he said as he stepped outside to get the patties off the grill. Walking back into the kitchen, he had a tray full of piping hot, well-done burgers ready to be assembled and devoured.

"Wow! Those look great!" she exclaimed and hopped off her stool. She grabbed a bun and began slathering on ketchup and mayonnaise.

"That would be interesting to have lived a completely different life," she said as she placed the patty, lettuce, tomato, and cheese on top of her bun.

"Yeah. I know, right?"

After she finished putting her burger together, he did the same.

Zax watched in anticipation as she put the burger in her mouth and chewed the first bite. He held his breath and hoped he would see her eyes sparkle again. But this time, not only did her eyes sparkle, her entire face glowed. She put her hand on her cheek and said, "Amazing!"

The momentary pride he felt quickly turned to bashfulness, and he did not know what to say. So, without saying a word, he simply pulled out his barstool, put his plate on the bar, and sat down next to her.

"I can't pretend anymore that the fries were just acceptable. They were the best I've ever had, and this is truly the best burger I've ever eaten. How did you get so good in one day?" she asked, taking another bite.

"Ha-ha. I'm a fast learner, that's all," he said gloating.

"Yeah, sure, whatever. You were probably an amazing cook before you got amnesia," she said. Zax chuckled at her comment. "But you still have one more course to get through, so don't start acting high and mighty now," she joked.

"No pressure," he said nervously.

"No pressure," she giggled and patted his shoulder.

For the last course, he'd decided to make a chocolate cake. He followed the recipe on the box by dumping the cake mix into a large bowl, adding eggs, water, and oil. He stirred for two minutes until it was thoroughly blended, poured it into a cake pan, and popped it in the oven. Thirty-five minutes later, it was ready for frosting.

He'd been uncertain about what flavor of frosting to spread on the cake, so he brought both chocolate and vanilla with him. He looked at both, trying to decide, and then had an idea. He spread the chocolate frosting over the entire cake with an icing spatula, then took the white frosting and added a message. Zax put the cake in front of Jaiden, and in white frosting, he'd written, "Sorry for breaking your phone."

Jaiden looked into his eyes and smiled sweetly. A few seconds later, they began to laugh at the awkwardness of the moment. Without saying a word, she picked up her fork and took a bite off the corner of the cake.

But as the cake touched her mouth, something supernatural seemed to happen. Zax looked in disbelief as she appeared, to him, to be melting like the witch from the Wizard of Oz while swirls of energy spiraled off her melting body. The swirls appeared to be identical to those coming off her phone and the traffic light. Zax thought maybe she was going to explode. He knew this couldn't actually be happening to Jaiden—or at least he hoped not. But it seemed so real. He wondered if she could see or feel what he was seeing? He panicked and stumbled backwards, knocking over his barstool. With his mind racing, he dropped his water on the floor and bolted out the front door.

Jaiden had no idea what was going on. Bewildered, she leaped from her barstool and chased Zax through the living room. She stopped at the edge of her porch and yelled, completely baffled, "Are you ok? What's wrong? Where are you going?"

Zax didn't say anything; he just kept running. Now, he saw swirls coming off everything around him. He ran all the way home. When he got there, he burst through the front door, charged up to his room, and jumped into bed. He was freaking out; he didn't like this feeling.

Jenny knocked on his door. "Zax?" she asked. He didn't answer. "Zax, what's wrong?" she asked more forcefully. He could tell she was concerned.

He still didn't answer. He closed his eyes tightly and covered his head. He wanted the swirls to go away; he didn't want to see the energy anymore.

13

Zax must have passed out because the next thing he knew, he was in a dark room and heard something quietly calling out his name. "Zax?"

As he began to wake up, the voice became louder and louder. "Zax, ZAX!" He opened his eyes to find Jaiden and Jenny in his room, calling his name.

He rubbed his eyes and wondered if he was dreaming.

"What's going on, Zax? Why did you run out of my house? I thought we were having a good time?" Jaiden asked with a combination of concern and anger. Zax convinced himself her concern outweighed the anger.

"How did you find my house?" he asked groggily.

"I went to her house to find out what happened, and I brought her here," Jenny said.

"So, why did you run out?" Jaiden asked again. Less concern this time.

"I don't know. I guess I've never had anyone treat me so nicely. It scared me," Zax said, hoping Jaiden would buy his explanation. He rolled over and turned his back to them. "I just want to sleep for now. I'll see you at school tomorrow, Jaiden."

Jenny and Jaiden looked at each other, puzzled. "Whatever," Jaiden said. "Guess I'll see you tomorrow." There was no question that all her concern was gone. Annoyance had completely taken its place.

Zax heard his bedroom door close followed by the muffled voices of Jaiden and Jenny in the hallway. He couldn't hear what they were saying, and he didn't care. All that mattered at this moment was that he was left alone to think. *What the hell is going on with me? What is this energy?*

The Detention

14

Zax's alarm clock went off Monday morning, waking him from a deep sleep. His stomach growled with hunger, and he realized that he'd not eaten anything since the day before at Jaiden's. He considered staying in bed, but the smell of bacon and eggs rising from the kitchen motivated him to get moving. Jenny's eggs were, without a doubt, worth getting up for.

Zax dreaded going back to school. The previous week had been a nightmare, and he was not looking forward to detention or dealing with idiots. But both awaited.

When he got to school, he found his name had been changed from "Caveman" to "the person that made us lose the big football game." He'd heard his new "name" blurted out at least a hundred times before first period. As he walked down the hall, even more kids than usual tried to trip him. Normally they would have succeeded, but for some strange reason, he could see it coming before it happened. He wasn't sure how, but it was pretty cool. He smiled as he walked around the jerks that tried.

15

Zax's favorite class was chemistry, and Mr. Carson had been his favorite teacher. But when Mr. Carson left for another school, all that changed.

With Mr. Carson's departure, Professor Brian—known to his students as Professor Evil—had somehow been hired by the schools brilliant Human Resources Department. Professor Brian was only five feet tall, had long white hair and brown eyes. He wore glasses that were too big for his face and had the demeanor of something akin to a demon. On top of that, he had a German accent that was difficult to understand at times. On the rare occasions when he looked up from his computer and spoke, his mumbled words seemed foreign. But not all his words. When he bragged about being a great scientist whose work had been rejected by the idiots in the scientific community—which he frequently did—his words were amazingly clear.

To make the nickname Professor Evil even more fitting, anyone in the class who dared to speak was slammed with an impossible homework assignment due the following day. The highest grade given to date on any of those assignments was 37. Zax wasn't sure who first called him Professor Evil, but they were correct in their labeling. How he got hired was one of the great mysteries of this school. From the moment Professor Brian first spoke, Zax seriously did not like him. And he believed the feeling was mutual.

Principal Hart was waiting by Zax's locker when the lunch bell rang and told him he needed to report to the chemistry lab for detention rather than the library. As luck would have it, the chess club decided to have an unscheduled meeting. Clearly, chess had priority over detention. Zax shut his locker door and wondered if this constituted cruel and unusual punishment. He could only hope that Professor Brian wasn't there. On his way to the lab, he passed Ms. Morgan's algebra classroom. Had this been the alternate location, he would have welcome detention and might have even tried for it again.

Zax sat down in the front seat of the second row of desks and opened his notebook. He didn't really know what he was supposed to do, but he assumed as long as he looked busy, he would be ok. He'd never been in detention before.

He was the only kid in the lab, and Professor Brian wasn't anywhere around. He tapped his pen on his desk. Looking around the empty room, he noticed a light radiating from Professor Brian's computer screen. It was on. So, like any curious student, he casually strolled over to take a look. After all, he was alone.

As Zax walked up to Professor Brian's desk, he had no idea what he would find on the oversized monitor. He hoped he might find some test questions or grades. But that wasn't what he found. Plastered on the computer screen was a news article headlined, "Intern Dies from Mad Scientist Brian's Experiment."

Zax's eyes widened and a lump developed in his throat. His mind immediately began racing faster than a supercomputer with random, frightening thoughts. He began to envision scenes in his mind of the professor performing experiments on him, with grotesque results. He ran back to his desk and grabbed his notebook. He hoped to get out before Professor Brian returned. He was two steps away from the door when Jaiden entered the room. He had somehow avoided her all day and hadn't seen her since she left his house.

"What are you doing in here?" Zax asked hastily.

"I came to give you some company and ask about yesterday," Jaiden said. Looking around the lab, she added, "Where's Professor Brian?"

Zax guessed she could sense his anxiety because before he could answer, she asked, "Are you ok?"

"Not really," he said with a frantic look in his eye. "We need to get out of here before he gets back!"

"Why? What happened?" she said, beginning to feel uneasy.

there, once again, looking at each other. No one knew what to say.

Like all the other recent times these bizarre things had happened, Zax ran out of the room as fast as he could, this time faster than ever. He felt terrible for leaving Jaiden, but he had to go. He didn't know what was going on with this energy, but he knew he should've stayed to make sure she was ok.

16

Zax ran home feeling as if he were about to throw up and pass out. He doubled over when he reached the front steps of his house and tried to catch his breath. He looked behind him to make sure no one was there. "*What* is going on?" he asked himself.

After he finally caught his breath, he went inside to find Jenny and Ethan changing a lightbulb. They asked why he was home early, and, like before, he told them everything. The troubled look on their faces alarmed him; it was a look he had never seen before.

Jenny reached out and grabbed his hand. "Zax, there's something…" A sudden knock at the door interrupted her confession. She dropped Zax's hand and turned to Ethan. "They're here," she whispered.

Ethan and Jenny tossed their chairs away from the living room wall and threw back the dark blue rug on which the chairs sat, revealing a secret panel in the floor. Zax froze as he watched them pry a single wood plank from the surrounding planks and grab a sniper rifle and pistol from the opening. He did not know what was happening, but as quickly as they reacted to the knock, it was apparent they had been expecting whoever was on the other side of the door to arrive.

"Stay here and don't move," Ethan whispered.

"Where did you get those guns?" Zax whispered back.

"Don't worry about that. Just go to your room," Jenny said quietly.

Zax quickly tiptoed up the stairs. He had just gotten into his room when he heard the front door being thrown open.

"Who are you? What do you want?" Ethan yelled with his pistol drawn. To his left, the barrel of Jenny's rifle rested on the overturned chair. She was ready to do what she had to do.

"I, uh..." It was Jaiden. "Please don't shoot," she quivered.

Zax charged out of his room, flew down the stairs and headed towards the front door.

"Stop! It's Jaiden!" he screamed as he raced down the hallway. "She's the friend that let me use her phone during lunch, and she was there when Professor Brian tried to attack me! Jenny, please put your gun down! You know her."

With his gun still pointed at Jaiden, Ethan turned to Jenny and asked, "You know her?"

"I do," Jenny answered, laying her rifle on the floor. "Put your gun away."

Ethan reluctantly lowered his gun but still gripped it tightly. Zax pushed him aside and got between him and Jaiden.

"Ethan, this is Jaiden," Zax said, hoping to ease everyone's tension. "Jaiden, this is Ethan. You already know Jenny."

"Wait, when did you meet her?" Ethan quizzed Jenny.

"Just this past weekend, but that's not important," Jenny replied.

The four of them stared at each other, seemingly afraid to speak. Finally, Jenny broke the ice. "Jaiden, would you like…"

"I'd like to talk to Jaiden alone," Zax interrupted. He took Jaiden's hand and led her outside, slamming the front door behind them.

"What was *that* all about?" Jaiden asked, still shaken up.

"I really don't know," Zax said, fuming, "but I *will* find out!"

He sighed and tried to calm himself. "I am *so sorry* about all of this," he said, motioning at the house, "but I promise you, I *will* find out!"

Jaiden poked his shoulder. "And what happened at school? You scared me in the chemistry lab. That teacher attacked you! You don't just run out when something like that happens!"

"I know. I'm really sorry. I didn't know what to do. That energy…" Zax's words trailed off, and he briefly looked at the ground before looking back at her. "How did you get out of there?"

"I ran out as soon as you did. Luckily, Coach Thomas was right outside the door," she said. "He stopped Professor Brian before he could harm me. I explained everything to him except for the energy part and then left as quickly as I could. When I left, Coach Thomas had called the authorities and was holding Professor Brian in his lab."

Zax was thankful that Coach Thomas happened to be outside the lab at just that moment. He didn't want to think about what could've happened if the Coach had gotten there even one second later.

After a few minutes of apologies and "it's ok's," Zax finally convinced Jaiden to go back inside with him. He understood her reluctance, but he felt she deserved answers as much as him.

They stepped inside the house and saw Ethan and Jenny sitting in the chairs they had tossed into the middle of the room. Jaiden and Zax stood in front of them.

Zax glared at his parents. "So, what happened?" he demanded. "I know this has something to do with the phone incident, and I think you owe me, I mean us, an explanation."

Jenny sighed and lowered her head. "It's time we tell you," she said.

"No! We can't tell him anything," Ethan said as he stood up and started pacing the floor.

"He has the right to know," Jenny pleaded.

"Tell me what?" Zax could feel his rage re-emerging.

"We can't tell him!" Ethan yelled.

"Why not? He needs to know. There's no reason to avoid telling him anymore," Jenny said forcefully. "Like you said, it won't go away."

"Avoid telling me what?" Zax quizzed and threw his hands in the air.

"We were ordered *never* to tell him, and you know it," Ethan said.

"That doesn't matter anymore. It's already been activated," Jenny remarked. She was not backing down.

"Activated what!!!" The anger in Zax's voice triggered the energy from earlier, and the energy surrounded him. With frightening intensity, it rushed towards Jenny and Ethan and aggressively slammed them backwards into the wall, shaking the house.

"What was that?" Jaiden shouted.

Zax froze. He couldn't believe what had just happened.

Ethan and Jenny lifted themselves off the floor. They both realized that the time had come to tell Zax the truth. All of it.

"We have to tell him," Jenny mumbled.

"Fine," Ethan said, "but remember that it wasn't my idea. I am *not* going to get in trouble for this."

"Whatever," Jenny said and turned to Zax. "So, you must have questions."

Zax stared at her for a few moments before he spoke. "What did I just do? Does it have to do with what happened with the phone and with Professor Brian's knife?" he asked.

Jenny sighed. "Yes, it does. The energy that, for years, was trapped inside of you was release because you came into contact with high-tech. In simple terms, the phone that Jaiden handed you provided a permanent gateway for you to release energy. That time, it was an uncontrolled release that overloaded and ultimately destroyed the phone," she said as if she'd rehearsed this response a thousand times.

"What energy are you talking about?" Zax asked.

"There's an energy in the core of the earth that —as far as we know—is only attracted to you. It travels through the mantel and the crust to the surface, where it's absorbed and stored in your body. Apparently, you have the ability to control this energy and use it as you see fit. Self-preservation seems automatic," she said matter-of-factly.

"Why is it attracted to me? And why didn't you tell me sooner?"

"We don't know why it's attracted to you. Once we learned about the energy at the core of three earth, a scanner was designed to trace the energy flow. The flow of energy led us to you. Further research indicated that you were unaware of the energy's attraction to you. Through trial and error, we learned that your contact with high-tech devices opened a gate for massive energy flow. Up until now, we have been able to keep the gateway closed, and you, unaware. Now, however, I'm afraid that the gate has been permanently opened. It didn't matter whether or not you knew about the energy as long as you were isolated from high-tech electronic devices," she said. "The origins of this energy are still unknown."

"But you were careless and did *not* do what you were told," Ethan snarled.

Incredible! Jaiden thought as she sat quietly listening. "What are you going to do now?" she asked, looking at Zax.

"I don't know," Zax shrugged. "This is all so confusing. Live life like always, I guess. Not really much to do other than try to learn how to control this energy."

Ethan turned and walked out of the room, disgusted. Jenny, Jaiden, and Zax stood in silence, not knowing how to move the current conversation along—or if they wanted to.

17

*B*AM, BAM, BAM!

The front door rattled and jolted them back to reality.

"Grab your gun, Jenny," Ethan whispered as he rushed back into the room and picked up his pistol. "You two, get back," he said, motioning to Zax and Jaiden.

Almost immediately, four SWAT looking dudes busted in, knocking the door off the hinges and shattering a living room window. Before Ethan and Jenny could react, the agents shot them with high voltage stun guns that knocked them unconscious. Jenny and Ethan didn't stand a chance to defend themselves. As much as Zax wanted Ethan to be knocked out, he'd always hoped it would be him who did it.

Zax held Jaiden behind him. He took a deep breath and saw the energy surround him like earlier. He thrust his hand in the direction of the SWAT team, and the energy flew across his arm at a blistering rate. To his surprise, he'd blasted them back through the front door and drilled them into the side of their cars.

"I can get used to this," Zax smirked.

The Revelation

18

Zax tried to create floating energy box-like containers to hold Ethan and Jenny, but they ended up looking more like some weird blob than a box. After that, he tried putting a layer of energy around Jaiden's entire body to protect her from bullets he feared might be coming their direction. Unfortunately, the most he could cover was her upper half. This being the case, he left her inside with Jenny and Ethan.

He stepped outside and saw three SWAT cars. The agents were nowhere to be found. Zax took another deep breath and began focusing on his right arm. The energy started to encompass his arm, and he punched towards the vehicles. The cars went flying into the air, then splashed into the lake and began to submerge.

The SWAT guys had managed to stumble to their feet and had crawled away from the cars before Zax had gotten outside. They'd taken cover behind Ethan's cryptic storage building. Zax could see their stun guns lying in the dirt. Confident these were not their only weapons, he closed his eyes and focused on harnessing the energy into something that would protect him from what he was sure was about to happen. It worked. A shield of energy, albeit oddly shaped, blocked every bullet from their .40 caliber pistols. Their attempt to blaze him up had failed. Silence replaced the gunfire. The agents were out of ammo.

They looked at their empty weapons and then back at Zax. They had only one choice—run to the woods for cover.

Zax thrust his arm out again, and another wall of energy went speeding in their direction. This energy wall literally picked them up and slammed them into the lake. Quickly they all recovered and began swimming to the other side.

Zax went inside and removed Jaiden's energy protection. With a little practice, he was able to maneuver the energy blobs that contained Jenny and Ethan around the room then outside the door. Fearing another SWAT team would arrive, they sprinted down the driveway and into the woods with Jenny and Ethan floating close behind.

"You can hide out at my house," Jaiden said once they stopped, trying to catch her breath.

"Why would you help me?" Zax asked, trying to do the same.

"In one day, you and I were attacked by a teacher and SWAT guys, and now I know you have this strange energy power thing. We're in this together. We're friends, and that's what friends do."

"Thanks, because we really don't have anywhere else to go," Zax sighed.

"How long can you keep them in the energy bubble?" Jaiden asked.

"I don't know, but I guess we'll find out. I just need to keep them alive," he said, looking at the blobs.

"You, Ethan, and Jenny can sneak through my window on the second floor. I have a pull-out couch you can sleep on," she said.

"This really means a lot." He paused, looking down. "Sorry for being such a burden."

"You're not a burden. It's not like you can do anything about this. It came out of nowhere for both of us. Besides," Jaiden smiled, "I thought this was going to be a boring place to live."

19

Jaiden led the way back to her house, taking a route that would keep them out of sight. Since Ethan and Jenny were still in the energy blobs, they could not afford to be seen.

Somehow, they made it. Once they arrived, Zax, Ethan, and Jenny hid in the backyard behind a row of hedges that stood around four feet tall.

"I've got to go in and talk to my mom for a sec. She's off work today. I'll open my bedroom window as soon as I get to my room," Jaiden said quietly. "That's it," she said, pointing to the window near the upper left corner of the house.

Zax nodded and watched as Jaiden took off. When he was confident she was inside, he poked his head around the corner of the hedges. It was just like he remembered from when he grilled burgers for her. Solid brick, two-story. One back door, several windows, all with closed blinds. The barbecue grill was still sitting to the right of the door. The only noticeable difference he detected was the addition of four lawn chairs—all different colors—sitting near the grill.

"That you, J?" Jaiden's mom yelled. Her voice was loud enough for Zax to hear. "What are you doing home? Did something happen at school?"

"School was fine. Just forgot about the early dismissal," Jaiden yelled back. "If it's ok, I'm going to take a nap."

"Ok," the faceless voice replied. "I'll call you for dinner if you're still asleep."

"Thanks," Jaiden replied.

Jaiden went to her room and locked the door behind her. The row of hedges was relatively close to the house, so there was no mistaking the sound of her opening the window.

Zax snuck up to the wall directly below Jaiden's window with the blobs of Ethan and Jenny at his side. He knew he had to try and develop a platform out of the energy. He straightened his arms in front of him and pointed them at his feet with his palms facing up. His first attempt failed miserably. The energy platform he created turned out to be the size of a frisbee and was not big enough for even one of his feet. He took a deep breath and tried again. This time the platform was about two feet in diameter. He lifted his arms in an upward motion, and the platform began to rise. But not for long. Halfway up the wall, it became unstable, and he plummeted back to the ground. He laid there for a minute—flat on his back and frustrated—until he saw Jaiden looking down, holding her hand over her mouth and laughing silently. *Guess it was kind of funny*, he thought.

Zax stood up, determined to make it work. He closed his eyes and focused on nothing other than the task at hand. He followed the same steps as before, but this time he kept his eyes closed in order to maintain his concentration. It worked. The platform floated him up to the window, and he crawled in. He then floated the energy blobs containing Ethan and Jenny up and maneuvered them through the window into the bedroom.

Other than the sleeper sofa, Jaiden's room had the same furnishings found in most bedrooms. It had a TV, a nightstand and, of course, a bed. Twin size. It was a bit unusual, however, in that she had painted the walls all different colors with random patterns. At a quick glance, Zax counted fourteen colors and seven painted shapes on the walls. There were also hand-drawn pictures thumbtacked everywhere. He assumed that she'd drawn them.

Zax suddenly felt exhausted. "If it's ok, I'm going to try and rest," he said. "I'll take the floor. Jenny and Ethan can have the sleeper. A lot has happened today, and I'm beat. Are you good with that?" he asked Jaiden.

She nodded and scanned her room. "Sorry there's not a lot of floor space, but try and make yourself comfortable." She walked to her closet and pulled out a lime green sleeping bag. "Maybe this will help. I know…"

"Jaiden, can you come down for a minute before your nap? I want to show you something," her mom's raspy voice yelled from downstairs. Zax couldn't help but wonder what she looked like.

"Ok," Jaiden yelled back. She lowered her voice to a near whisper. "I have to go see what she wants, but I'll be back in a few minutes."

When the door shut behind Jaiden, Zax quietly unfolded the bed inside the sofa. He positioned Jenny and Ethan—who were still floating—above the bed and slowly lowered them while removing the energy bubbles. He unrolled the sleeping bag, grabbed an oversized stuffed panda off Jaiden's bed, and put it on the floor to use as a pillow. Once his head hit the panda, he immediately passed out.

20

"Zax, Zax, ZAX!!!" An ominous voice echoed in his head.

He was in a dark room again. But this time, a small light appeared. It grew and grew until it was all that could be seen. The blinding light forced Zax to open his eyes, and he woke up seeing Ethan's face. It was just a dream, but he felt like there was more to it.

Zax looked around and saw three sandwiches on a paper plate. *Must have been dinner*, he thought. Jaiden was nowhere to be seen. He glanced at the clock on the wall. It was 6:30 am. *Have I been asleep that long?*

"Where are we? What happened?" Ethan asked and sat up on the side of the sofa bed, rubbing his head.

"We're at Jaiden's house. You and Jenny were knocked unconscious by high powered tasers that were shot by some SWAT dudes. They knocked you out; then I knocked them out. Gave them a run for their money," Zax boasted as he stood up. "We snuck over to Jaiden's to hide. Are you ok?"

"I am, but I don't remember anything after the SWAT team rammed through our door." Ethan paused briefly and reached down to take Jenny's hand. "She's still unconscious; hopefully, she'll wake up soon and be ok," he mumbled. "She has to. Headquarters has a lot of explaining to do."

Ethan had a frightened look on his face. Even though he tried to hide it, Zax could tell he was afraid. The last time he saw this look on Ethan was when a spider was crawling on his arm. Ethan didn't like spiders much. To tell the truth, he didn't like them at all.

Zax was worried for Ethan and Jenny right now. Despite the fact that he and Ethan had never gotten along very well, Ethan was still his dad. And they *were* his family, the only family he had.

"Wait a minute. Do you or Jenny have this power too?" Zax asked. "I mean, I must have inherited it somehow."

Ethan stood up and walked to the window. With his back to Zax, he said, "Um, about that. I guess if you know about the energy, then you should know..."

"Know what?" Zax asked, interrupting his sentence.

Ethan turned back to Zax and looked him in the eye. He hoped he was about to do the right thing. "Jenny and I are not your parents. Much of what we've told you in the past is...well...it isn't true. I don't actually work for the phone company and Jenny is not actually a stay-at-home mom. We're agents for a top-secret organization. We were assigned to watch you and make sure you didn't get out of control," he paused. "I'm sorry, Zax."

Zax was not sure he comprehended what Ethan had just told him. "What are you talking about? What do you mean you're not my parents? What organization? What do you mean 'out of control'?" Zax asked quickly, without giving Ethan a chance to answer any of his questions.

"The energy was so unstable," Ethan said. "We weren't sure if you could keep it from going crazy. I know this is a lot to process..."

Ethan continued to talk, but Zax couldn't hear anything other than a muffled, indistinct voice. His head was spinning. All he could do was stand and stare at whoever this person was that stood in front of him.

Finally, Zax snapped out of his trance. Ethan was still talking, but Zax interrupted. "How did you find me? How did you know I had this power?" With each word, his whisper became more intense. It took all he had to keep his voice down so that Jaiden's parents wouldn't hear him.

Ethan shuffled back to the sofa bed and sat on the corner. "Many years ago, our scientists developed a scanner that could measure energy levels all the way to the center of the earth. As a result, they discovered a huge energy source in the core and began closely monitoring it. The scanner seemed to indicate that the energy followed a single path to the surface. That path led us directly to you. Jenny and I were part of the team that found you suffering from a coma in a hospital bed. Someone found you unconscious in an alley and brought you to the nearest medical facility. The doctors didn't know what caused you to go into a coma. But, as soon as we got to the hospital, you woke up. All other details about you were kept confidential and not shared with us. The director wanted to quarantine you in a storage facility hundreds of feet underground, but Jenny and I intervened. She convinced the director to let us take custody of you. You had no recollection of what happened before the coma. They said it was amnesia, but it was more like a part of your brain was being cut off, like you couldn't access it. As if something was blocking you from seeing your memories."

Zax sat down on Jaiden's bed and buried his face in his hands, almost crying. *I have no family and nowhere to go. I'm alone. All by myself*, he thought.

"So, I'm alone," he said despondently and looked back at Ethan.

"No, Zax, you're not. Once Jenny convinced the director to let you live with us, you became part of our family. And your friend Jaiden, she's here for you too. You are *not* alone," Ethan said and stood up. "You'll never be alone."

Zax sat for another moment, filled with torment, then got up and gave Ethan a big, long hug. "I'm scared," he said softly and held Ethan tightly.

This was the first time in his life he felt he ever needed—or wanted—Ethan's support.

"We all are, but you have to be brave from now on, ok? We all have to."

A rush of fear flooded through Zax, and he pulled away from Ethan. "Wait. Can they trace us here?" he stammered.

"Yes, but it takes at least two days to recharge the current scanner. They were probably monitoring you when you fought the agents. If that's the case, we have some time."

"Why are they after me?" Zax asked.

Ethan sighed. "They are…"

"Where are we?" Jenny interrupted, rolling over on the sofa bed. She looked as confused as Ethan had when he first woke up. "What happened? And why aren't we at home?"

Before Ethan could finish answering Zax or begin answering Jenny, Jaiden walked in.

"You're up. Are you guys ok?" Jaiden asked.

"Yeah," Zax said, trying to regain his composure. "We're good." Zax looked back at Ethan with a somber face. "So, what do we do now?"

"You're going to school," Ethan said. "They won't risk the lives of students. Hopefully, anyway."

"What about you and Jenny?" Zax asked.

"We're going to try to convince the director not to quarantine you. It'll be hard, but not impossible,"

Ethan said. The look on his face made it seem like this would be more challenging than it sounded.

"Can someone please tell me what's going on?" Jenny asked sluggishly.

Ethan sat down beside her and told her everything that had happened.

"So, we go to the director, and Zax just goes to school? What about his teacher? Professor Brian?" Jenny asked, still trying to wake up enough to grasp what was going on.

"He's not a problem," Jaiden said. "I looked online, and the headline of the local newspaper was "School Teacher Fired and Arrested for Attacking Students." They said Professor Brian was a nut and that there was some sort of energy coming off one of the kids who was attacked, or something like that." She nudged Zax. "We need to get to school. You ready?"

"Yeah. I'll be there in a sec." Zax looked at Ethan and Jenny. "I have to go. Are you two going be ok?"

"We'll be fine. We're going to head back to the house for a quick shower and a change of clothes, then we're going to check in with the director and bring him up to date on our situation," Ethan said.

"I'll meet you at the house after school, then?" Zax asked.

Jenny stood up weakly. "We'll be waiting," she said. She reached down and took Zax's hand in hers. "Try not to worry. I'm quite sure we'll get to keep you.

I don't think the director will change his mind after all these years." She touched the side of his cheek. *I hope not, anyway,* she thought. "Everything will be fine, I promise."

"Try not to let your power slip out in public. We don't need anyone else knowing about you," Ethan added.

21

Zax and Jaiden got to school, and it seemed like any other day—as if nothing had happened. But so much had. In the past twenty-four hours, they had been attacked by a teacher and a SWAT team, they found out Zax controlled a powerful energy, and they learned of a secret organization. The only good thing that came out of the dreadful day was that Zax knew he could now easily knock out the kids who made fun of him or called him Caveman. And knowing that was enough. The thought of punching them through the roof was so nice, but he was better than that. *I could, but no,* he thought as he ignored the bullies.

Zax was on his way to detention when Jack snuck up behind him and said, "You will pay for what you did to me."

Zax spun around and saw a cast on Jack's arm. *I didn't know I threw him that hard at the wall,* he thought. Zax stared at him with a "you need to back up before I break your other arm" look, and Jack backed up. *Yes, I could punch him through the wall, but no, that would just get me in more trouble. He's not worth it,* Zax thought.

Zax took a few steps in Jack's direction and purposely bumped into his arm, letting him know he wasn't afraid. Jack stumbled backwards into a display case, and a silent look of pain came across his face. Once Jack regained his footing, he was furious. He raised his fist to punch Zax but stopped when he realized the arm he lifted was the broken one. *Idiot*, Zax thought. *But I do feel bad about breaking his arm.*

About that time, Jaiden walked up. Upon seeing her, Jack turned and stomped away.

"What was that all about?" Jaiden asked.

"Nothing," Zax said. "Let's just forget about it."

22

After school, they walked back to Zax's old house and found Ethan and Jenny making temporary repairs to the door and window that the SWAT team had damaged. "Are you thinking we can stay here?" Zax asked. "Should you be working this hard after last night?"

"We're fine," Jenny said. "We rested most of the morning, then went to the agency to talk to the director. And..." she paused and looked down.

"And what?" Zax felt his heart fall to his feet.

Jenny raised her head and looked directly at Zax. "Well, he didn't say no. He said he would consider letting you stay with Ethan and me and give us an answer soon. He also said he would *not* send any more agents to try and take you in while he considers the request."

Zax lowered his head and looked down at his feet, clearly disappointed. *At least things are stable for the moment*, he thought. He looked back up, sat his backpack on the ground, and asked, "What can we do to help?"

23

With Zax's future in limbo and not being able to have lunch with Jaiden at school, the next two weeks seemed to pass dreadfully slow. But detention was finally over, and things were starting to return to normal. At school, anyway.

Everyone was still talking about Professor Brian. The internet widely reported that he'd been arrested and returned to prison, but details were sketchy. Coach Thomas was praised for his quick thinking and bravery. Strangely, none of the reports mentioned Zax or Jaiden's name.

Zax and Jaiden went back to having lunch together and had begun spending more time with each other after school. It turned out they had a lot in common, like frozen yogurt and sci-fi books.

Whenever he and Jaiden weren't together, Zax studied and worked on controlling his new energy. He knew he could deflect bullets, but he wondered what else he could do. When he was alone, he practiced making energy bubbles and modifying them for various uses. Specialty equipment seemed easy to make—guns, not so much.

The Chupacabra

24

The following Wednesday, Jack again slipped up behind Zax as he was walking down the hall. Zax felt his presence and turned quickly to face him. "Why do you keep doing this?" Zax asked.

Jack was caught off guard, surprised by Zax's quick reaction. "Look what you did to my arm. And it's all your fault. My life is ruined!" he said, waving his cast at Zax.

Zax knew Jack was right; it was his fault. An idea flashed into his head.

Zax reached out and touched Jack's arm. He funneled a light burst of energy through his cast, hoping that somehow this would speed up the healing process. He wasn't sure if it would work, but the puzzled look on Jack's face told him it had. It was obvious that Jack was no longer in pain.

"What the…" Jack said, looking directly at his arm. Zax had taken a gamble, and it paid off. Even though Jack was a jerk and a bully, he was glad he did it.

Zax grinned at the shock on Jack's face, but before he could say anything, a deafening rumble permeated through the wall. At first, Zax thought it was an earthquake. But he was wrong.

Suddenly, the solid brick wall came crashing in, and a monstrous, green, scaly creature came pummeling through. All Zax could see was the front half of the beast. It had the body of a snake, the hide of a crocodile, the legs of a Komodo dragon, and the head of a mythical dragon. Purple horns protruded from the sides of its head, and its vicious mouth had teeth larger than half of a normal human.

Terrifying screams came from every direction as students, teachers, and staff scrambled to get away. Zax stumbled over the debris and fell inches from the beast. For him, there was no escape.

The beast grabbed for Zax, and Zax raised his arms, trying to block its attack. He instantly realized that he wasn't being crushed and that a dome of energy covered him. He didn't remember summoning the energy for the dome, but it completely surrounded him, protecting him from the beast.

Zax stood up—still covered by the energy—and tried to come up with a plan. He knew he was going to need something more than just pushed energy to defeat this monster. Its teeth were massive, and its body was so long and lanky, that he had to keep his distance.

The beast was relentless and had, thus far, been unsuccessful in its attempts to crash through the energy dome to get to Zax. But that changed in an instance. A hairline crack began to form right in front of Zax's face, and he knew he had to figure out what to do before the dome shattered and crumbled around him.

He knew he needed a tool of some kind, something long. But before the energy could form into anything, the beast broke through the dome. He slammed Zax into the wall at the end of the hallway with his snout, and Zax flew backwards and crashed to the floor. The energy had lessened the severity of the impact, but to Zax, it still really hurt.

Zax sat dazed for a moment, but as the beast spun around and charged towards him, he searched its body for a weak spot. The only vulnerability he could see was right between its eyes. It was the only place on the beast's body that was not covered with a thick hide.

Zax started feeling like something powerful was beginning to bubble up inside him, something more intense than the energy he was accustomed to. This stronger energy began to form around his hand, but it felt entirely different. It was more concentrated. Zax felt as though this new energy could kill the beast in one push.

He stood up and tried pushing the energy towards the beast, but nothing happened. The energy began to transform. It started stretching out and looked like a long arrow before finally taking the form of a spear.

As the beast scrambled towards him, Zax hastily threw the energy spear—aiming for the weak spot.

The spear bounced off the beast's incredibly strong hide; he'd missed.

Zax knew he had to get closer to the beast if he hoped to eliminate it. He climbed up onto a pile of rubble and jumped down directly in front of its head. Unexpectedly, the beast opened its mouth and exposed jagged, razor-sharp teeth. There was no way for him to reach the spot without being sucked in.

Realizing this, Zax leaped and sprung off one of the beast's fangs. Quickly he sent a burst of energy to the bottom of his feet. The burst pushed him to the floor and, at the same time, propelled the beast upward. The weak spot on the beast's head slammed hard into the ceiling. A loud scream echoed from its mouth as it twisted and turned violently, then backed out of the building.

Zax followed it out and could now see its full body. Its body was super long and had four more Komodo dragon feet. As he studied the beast, he had another idea with regards to taking it out.

He ran under the beast and threw the spear at it, straight up. The beast dodged it, but Zax knew that what goes up, must come down. He did a cocky point to the sky, and surprisingly, the beast looked up. The spear turned, came down, went straight through its weak spot, and continued through its entire body, killing it instantly. The colossal beast crashed to the ground and evaporated into a purple dust that blew into the wind. There was nothing left except the spear. Zax took a minute to catch his breath.

Great. Now I have even more questions. Where did this thing come from? Why did it attack me? Zax stood outside, watching the purple dust settle, and tried to wrap his head around what had just taken place. There were no easy answers.

25

With all the confusion and chaos, school was immediately dismissed for the day. Principal Hart said he was determined to figure out what happened, but Zax knew he, nor anyone, would be able to make sense of it. Since no one was injured, the media quickly lost interest. A damage assessment was begun.

Ethan and Jenny were painting the front window frame when Zax and Jaiden arrived. It was the final touch in repairing the window that had been broken by the SWAT team.

"Hey," Zax said. "Looks like you're busy."

"We're just finishing up," Ethan said, putting the lid on the paint can.

"Guess what?" Jenny asked excitedly. "We called the agency, and you don't have to be quarantined. You can stay with us!"

"Really?" Zax asked, somewhat shocked. But in a good way.

"Yes! And we made sure they would *never* send any more agents to try and take you in. Plus..." she smiled and turned to Ethan, "we get to move to a house in town!"

"Are you serious?"

"Yep," Ethan said. "There is one catch, however. You will have to work with us at the agency when you're available. Work will consist of physical training, learning to control the energy, paperwork, and anything else the director wants."

"Ok. I can do that. Why not? It won't be too hard," Zax said cautiously.

"You say that, but the agents you threw in the water are really, really angry and might give you a hard time. Wait a minute," Ethan said and looked at his watch. It was 2:02. "What are you doing out of school?"

Zax and Jaiden looked at each other, not knowing where to start.

"Let's go inside," Jaiden finally said. "I'll make some coffee, and Zax can tell you everything."

Ethan and Jenny turned their attention back to Zax and saw an apprehensive look on his face. He knew he had to tell them—not like he could keep it a secret—but he wished he didn't have to do it right now.

26

Starting with his encounter with Jack, Zax explained everything that had happened in full detail. After hearing the whole story, Ethan and Jenny admitted that they had no idea where the monster came from.

"Tell you what," Ethan said, taking his last sip of coffee, "how about we go ahead and take a drive down to the agency, and you can check it out. Maybe they will know something about this creature."

Zax sat in the backseat of Ethan and Jenny's silver Honda Accord and stared out the window as they made the trek to work. Having never worked before, he was looking forward to whatever challenge awaited him. Within reason, of course.

As they pulled into the parking lot, Zax struggled to believe this was where he would be working. He didn't know what he had expected, but this type of building never entered his realm of consideration, especially after the long, gravel road that led to its location.

The four-story structure was encased in opaque reflective glass, had solar panels covering the flat roof, and two solid oak doors with a keypad. An intriguing yellow logo was in the center of the right door. There were no windows or identifying markers as to what was housed inside. A small metal sign staked in the ground read "Four Tower Plaza." Nothing else.

"What do you think?" Jenny asked as she unbuckled her seatbelt.

"Pretty cool building," Zax said.

Ethan punched in the entry code and motioned for Zax to go in. "Zax, remember what I told you, these guys were humiliated and are *really* mad at you. The director has turned them loose. They have guns, so be prepared."

No sooner than Zax's right foot crossed the threshold, bullets started flying at him from all directions. But the bullets never touched him; without even being aware, he had made an energy shield and had successfully deflected every one of them. Ethan was right; clearly, these agents were furious. But they were no match for him. *Seriously? Didn't they learn the first time at our old house,* he thought.

When the bullets stopped, Zax stepped further into the building, followed by Ethan and Jenny.

"Good job," Ethan whispered in Zax's ear. "But keep in mind that these agents will constantly be testing your capabilities when you're here. You'll just have to use your energy, as necessary, to stop whatever they send your way without losing control."

"Easy for you to say. You don't have people trying to kill you. At least that's what it looks like to me," Zax said, staring at the room full of agents. He turned to Ethan and asked, "Wait, will you and Jenny try to kill me too?"

"No, we would never do that. Even if we tried, I'm sure you could easily stop us."

Zax relaxed a bit and smiled. The room in which they stood was nothing more than a large, undecorated foyer with cameras mounted in all four corners. There was one desk in the middle which seemed to be normally unoccupied. In the center of the back wall was a heavy security door. A card reader and keypad were on the adjacent wall. This door apparently provided access to other areas of the building.

"Does this place have anything to do with the creature I battled earlier today at school?" Zax asked.

About that time, the security door clicked open, and in walked a slightly overweight, balding man who, unlike everyone else, was wearing a suit and tie.

"We call it a Chupacabra. We don't know where it came from, but we discovered it when we did a scan to look for you this morning," the deep-voiced man said as he walked towards Zax. "It showed up as a large, slow-moving energy blip."

"Zax, this is the director. He's the boss," Ethan said.

"You will call me 'mister' or 'sir.' To make things perfectly clear, you are the biggest annoyance I have. If you create any problems for me—

whatsoever—it will be me that takes you out," the director said.

He stood in front of Zax, trying to assert his authority. A few seconds later, he pulled a gun from his shoulder holster and placed it against Zax's forehead. Zax stepped back, away from the gun, but the director kept up. Once again, a spear began to form in Zax's hand. Using the spear, he pushed the director's hand into the air and tossed it at the gun. The spear seemed to be absorbed into the gun and disappeared. Zax thought the spear was a dud until the gun began to glow and overflow with energy, just like Jaiden's phone. The director dropped the gun as it became hot. Then, the light just faded away.

The director smiled. "Hope you didn't damage my gun." He looked towards one of the agents. "Bring that gun to my office when it cools down," he instructed. He turned and headed back to the security door. "See you soon, Zax. You better stay out of trouble."

I don't think I'm going to like him, Zax thought watching the director walk away.

Zax returned his gaze to the crowd of agents. As he scanned their unsettled faces, they began to back up. *I don't think I have much to worry about. I honestly don't know how I do so well with this energy, having just unleashed it. It feels like I've had it my entire life. Seems so natural, like a reflex or something*, he thought.

Ethan tapped Zax on the shoulder, breaking his train of thought. "How about a quick tour, then we'll head home. I think you'll get the hang of everything here soon enough."

"Ok, I need to study for a test anyway."

As they headed for the security door, Zax turned back around and, with the craziest face he could make and in his creepiest voice, said, "See everyone later. Good luck trying to kill me before I kill you."

Everyone remaining in the room backed up a step or two.

Zax turned back and followed Ethan and Jenny. *Of course, I'm not going to kill them; just a little payback for the bullets. This is gonna be fun!* he thought.

Driving home, Zax could not help but wonder what to expect once he officially started work. He wasn't sure what he could possibly do to help in an office where agents were challenged to kill him. But, he thought, having a new house in town and not being quarantined, made it worth finding out.

The Field Trip

27

The day after the battle with the Chupacabra, school reopened. Everything looked the same except for the barricaded, gaping hole in the hallway and the presence of onsite construction workers. Principal Hart still had no answers, and all the kids disagreed about what they had seen. By noon, talk of the beast had diminished considerably. Weirdly, no one seemed to connect Zax with the incident.

During last period, Zax's history class was told of an upcoming exam. His teacher usually came up with an incentive to get the kids to study, like going to an amusement park or having a pizza party or something like that. This time, however, it was a trip to the beach in San Diego, California. Zax had never been to a beach, and although he really wanted to go, he doubted that the director, Ethan, or Jenny would let him. Whatever the case, he decided it was worth a shot to ask.

Ethan and Jenny picked Zax up at school for the first time, so when everyone saw him get into a car, they stared at him, confused and surprised. *Maybe this will keep me from being bullied all the time,* he thought. *But I doubt it.*

Once Zax closed the car door and was buckled in, he asked sheepishly, "So, Ethan, Jenny, is there anything that I can do for you once we get home?"

Ethan looked at him suspiciously. "Ok, Zax. What do you want?"

"What are you talking about? Can't I simply do something for the people who kept me from being quarantined hundreds of miles underground? The people that took care of me for all these years?"

"You can," Jenny smiled, "but I'm guessing you want something in return."

"Is it that obvious?" Zax grinned.

"Yes, so what do you want?" Ethan asked, looking at him in the rearview mirror.

"If I pass my history exam, there's a school trip that I can go on. It's to San Diego."

"San Diego! I love San Diego!" Jenny exclaimed. She paused and turned around to look at him. "Wait. Did you say San Diego? As in California? That's a long way from here."

Zax looked down. "I know, but…"

"I don't care as long as you study hard, pass the test, and control the energy. I'm perfectly fine with it," Ethan interrupted before Zax could finish pleading his case.

Did I hear this right? Ethan is ok with me going if I study and pass? he thought, surprised. *No way he just said it was ok.*

"I'm ok with it, too," Jenny said. "The challenge is going to be convincing the director to let you go and figuring out how to pay for it."

Zax was dumbfounded. He had no words to describe the conversation that had just taken place.

"We're here," Ethan said as he pulled into the driveway of their new house. "The movers moved the kitchen and bedroom furniture today, so we can spend the night here. They should be able to finish up tomorrow."

The boxy, blue two-story house had shutters on the windows, a two-car garage, and a white front door. The yard was small, and if anyone scanned the street, they'd have trouble telling one house from the other. Jaiden's house was now only three blocks away. Things were definitely looking up.

Ethan unlocked the front door, and he, Jenny, and Zax went in. As they stepped inside, it appeared to be like most of the other houses that Zax had been in. It had a kitchen, living room, dining room, bedrooms, and bathrooms. But there was more to it. Much more. And he was about to find out just how unique this one-of-a-kind home was.

After checking out his bedroom and grabbing a bottle of root beer from the refrigerator, Ethan led Zax to a hidden stairway tucked inside the pantry. The narrow, dimly lit stairway led to a warehouse-sized basement with two levels. It had top-notch security, an exercise room with the latest equipment, an entire room of nothing but guns, a room for virtual training, a shooting range and a frozen yogurt bar.

"This is awesome!" Zax exclaimed. "How did all this get here?"

"Secretly built. Don't worry about that," Ethan said. "We want you will train in the virtual training room before being instructed on how to use a gun."

"Then I can take a break and have some frozen yogurt, right?"

"No, then you will do your homework and study for your test," Jenny said, joining them.

"It won't matter if the director doesn't let me go on the trip," Zax replied.

"Maybe he will, maybe he won't. You never know," she said, shrugging her shoulders. "But after you study, you can have some frozen yogurt."

"Deal!" Zax said and shook her hand.

Zax loved frozen yogurt; it was his favorite dessert in the world. The frozen creaminess with all the different toppings and different flavors, he just loved it.

Ethan and Zax went into the virtual training room to test it out. Inside the training room was a control room whereby Ethan could select a situation and set the difficulty level. Once selected, the training room immediately turned into that situation.

"Let's start small," Ethan said as he pressed buttons on a large touchscreen monitor. "A bank robbery." He turned to Zax and warned, "Remember, don't injure anyone you don't need to. Learn how to control your energy and not let it get out of hand."

"I know what I'm doing," Zax said confidently.

The hologram started, and he was in the middle of a completely different room. He was inside a bank where people were tied up and lying on the ground. He guessed these were hostages and that the people standing around with guns and ski masks were most likely the robbers. Two armed men were by the door, one was with the banker, and three with the hostages.

Zax put a barrier of energy around the hostages to protect them from bullets. It was supposed to have smooth edges, but these were rough. They were not like the blob he created when picking up Jenny and Ethan.

The robbers started shooting at Zax. He raised his hands in the same way he did with Professor Brian and the Chupacabra. The bullets stopped in midair, and he directed them into the wall before creating a cage of energy around the robbers. As quickly as the room, the robbers, and the hostages appeared, they disappeared. The ceiling lights popped on, and a sign lit up above the control room door that said: "Passed."

"Good job!" Ethan said. "You protected the civilians first, then surrounded the robbers."

"It wasn't hard at all," Zax said.

"That was the easiest setting. Next time I'll put it on the hardest setting if you want. It involves a dragon."

"You know what, I'll just do the second easiest next time," Zax said, smiling.

Ethan smiled back. "Ok, let's go see Jenny for the gun lesson."

They left the hologram room and descended another set of stairs to the soundproof gun range located on the lowest level of the house. Inside the concrete room were five divided shooting lanes; each had a pistol and a magazine in a lockbox, earmuffs, and shooting glasses. At the far end of each lane, a retractable silhouette target hung from a railing attached to the ceiling.

Jenny was standing next to the row nearest the door when Zax and Ethan entered the room.

"Look at this place!" Zax said in awe of the shooting range. "Can't wait to learn how to shoot a pistol."

"That's how most everyone feels the first time they see a range. Pretty exciting, huh?" Jenny asked.

"Yeah, pretty exciting."

"I doubt that bullets will be very effective against monsters like the Chupacabra," she quipped, "but we think you need to know how to use one just in case."

"I think that's a great idea," Zax said, still awestruck over the fact that his house had a gun range.

"Before I can let you shoot, I need to go over some safety procedures with you, teach you how to properly hold a gun, and make sure you're fully aware of the responsibilities that come with gun ownership and use."

"Sounds reasonable. Let's do it."

For forty-five minutes, Jenny went through the safety guidelines set in place by the NRA, showed him how to securely grip his weapon, and told him what to expect once the gun discharged.

"Remember," Jenny said as Zax picked up the pistol, "earmuffs and glasses first. And make sure you use both hands to hold the gun because it will kick. If you miss the target, readjust your position, and you'll likely hit closer the next time."

Zax followed protocol. He positioned his hands on the gun as instructed, looked down the range, and put his site on the target. He squeezed the trigger gently and shot. Zax's hands flew straight up. *Boy, was she talking about a kick!* he thought. He missed the target but quickly repositioned himself and fired again. This time the bullet nicked the right corner. On the third try, he hit the target dead center.

"Way to go!" Jenny said, clapping her hands. After shooting for another half hour and hitting the target near the bullseye most every time, Jenny told him what a great job he'd done but that it was time for him to go study.

"Do I really need to?"

"If you want to go on the trip and get some frozen yogurt, you certainly do."

"Fine. I'll go study in my room," Zax said as he turned and looked proudly at the targets.

Now came the hardest task of the day, studying. He wasn't sure he would make it out alive, but he would definitely do his best to get some frozen yogurt.

Zax climbed back up the three flights of stairs to his bedroom. He was just about to grab his history book from his backpack when, yet again, he was in a dark room, much like the one from Jaiden's house.

"Zax," a soft voice called out.

Zax squinted and looked around, but no one was there. He felt his heart skip a beat. Confused and somewhat unsettled, he quietly asked, "Wh-who are you?"

"I am you, just like you are me," it said.

Zax stood silently for a moment, trying to grasp what was going on. "I'm not sure I understand," he said. After a brief pause, he asked, "Wait, are you the energy?"

"Yes. You are smarter than I thought," the unseen voice replied.

"What is that supposed to mean?"

"Nothing," the energy continued. "For now, this is the only way for us to talk. I can tell you everything about yourself, like where you really came from and how you became who you are, but right now, you need to wake up and protect those who can't protect themselves."

"Wait! You can't tell me you know everything about me, then just leave!" Zax yelled.

"In time, you will know. But they need you now. Wake up, Zax," the energy said as its voice faded away.

Zax woke up wondering if this was just a dream. But considering the way his life had changed since he'd discovered the energy, he doubted that was the case.

28

The next morning, Zax told Jenny and Ethan what happened the night before and about his encounter with the energy.

"That's strange," Jenny said.

"How do you know it was the energy? It could've simply been a dream," Ethan said. His usual, unpleasant tone had returned.

"I'm not sure. It just felt like a part of me, like it has been a part of me my entire life."

Jenny and Ethan stared at him.

"It's going to be ok; I'm *not* going crazy," Zax said. He was clearly irritated. He grabbed his backpack and headed for the front door. "I need to go. See you after school." With that, he was off to school and his history test.

29

Zax had studied hard for the test and was confident he would pass. It took him forty-three minutes, but he finished with ease. Results were not going to be posted until early next week, yet he was certain it was safe to begin packing. At least from the standpoint of passing the test. The challenge now was to get approval from the director.

Since history was his last class of the day, Zax was free to leave campus after the test. Ethan had suggested that he stop by the office after school and find out what he would be doing over the weekend. The problem was that Jenny and Ethan were both busy, and it was a three-mile walk to the agency. He thought for a minute and came up with an idea. He went behind the gym and decided to experiment with his energy. He looked around to make sure no one could see him, then constructed a small platform beneath his feet. This time, however, rather than raising his arms upward to elevate him, he swung his arms behind him, much like he would move his foot if he were on a skateboard. It worked. He grinned as the energy board took off in the direction of the agency—skimming just above the ground. "So cool," he said. "Maybe one day I'll be able to fly."

Fifteen minutes later, he arrived at the agency for the second time. *Surely they learned their lesson,* he thought as he punched in the entry code that Ethan had given him. Zax opened the heavy door, and literally everyone had a gun on him—again. Bullets began flying in his direction from everywhere, and once again, he deflected them with an energy shield. *Unbelievable!* he thought. *How do they know I'm coming?*

Just as Zax was about to lower his shield, one final bullet headed his way. But rather than deflecting to the ground, the bullet ricocheted back in the direction of one of the agents. Zax threw a shield of energy around the agent, but the bullet then ricocheted back in Zax's direction and zipped right past his head.

"You need to stop this!" Zax yelled. "That man almost got himself killed. It's pretty obvious that I have control over the energy."

"That's his job," the director said, stepping into the foyer through the security door as the gunfire ceased. "His job is to protect the world from you even if it means putting his life on the line. What if you lose control in the future?"

"I won't lose control. Even if I did, how will you kill me in the future if you can't kill me now?"

The director looked at Zax angrily and stormed off like a ten-year-old. The room grew silent, and after a minute, everyone went back to work.

A stocky, brown-eyed agent with short brown hair and a narrow mustache approached Zax and led him into a brightly lit room with a large conference table covered in papers. "Zax, I'm Agent Morrison. I'm glad you stopped by. This is the mission room where we plan our operations."

A hologram popped up as they neared the table. It was like the training room at the house, but rather than fill the room, it simply hovered above the table. This hologram, however, was a beach with a rainstorm and giant waves heading toward it.

"What's this? I don't get it," Zax said to Agent Morrison.

"Remember the Chupacabra? Once we learned about how the Chupacabra attacked you, we did an energy scan to try to determine where it came from. Although the scan was inconclusive, we did determine that the Chupacabra was infused with an energy like nothing we had seen before. The energy that is building in the wave shown in this hologram is similar in nature to that same energy. The waves seem to be growing larger and more threatening, and we think they will peak next week on the beach near San Diego, California. Due to the similarities of the energies, we think you should check it out."

"Really? I have a field trip to the same place with my history class," Zax said. *This is really weird*, he thought. *What are the odds? Is this really a coincidence, or could someone or something be trying to spoil the trip to San Diego for Jaiden and me?*

"That's great news. The field trip will be the perfect cover. And because you'll be working part of the time, we'll pay all your expenses," Agent Morrison said.

"Are you serious?" Zax exclaimed.

He couldn't believe Agent Morrison just said they would pay for the trip. He'd been wondering how he was going to pay for it. He doubted that Ethan and Jenny could afford it, and he knew his meager paycheck wouldn't cover it.

"I *am* serious. And..." Agent Morrison said, pushing away from the table, "we have another thing for you."

"Oh, ok. What?" Zax couldn't imagine what could possibly top them paying for his trip.

"After killing the Chupacabra and considering your abilities to control the energy and use it to protect people, some of us now think you qualify as...let's say a superhero, for lack of a better word. Therefore," he said, walking towards the closet in the room, "we made you your very own superhero suit, complete with white gloves and white boots. And with this on, no one will know you are associated with the office."

"No way, man," Zax laughed, shaking his head.

Agent Morrison reached in the closet and pulled out a blue bodysuit. It had a yellow lightning bolt on the chest, white stripes down the sides of the torso and the legs, and a Zorro-like mask that tied around his head. The openings in the mask for his eyes were covered by a see-through white material. He held it up for Zax to examine, then pulled out a small, compartmentalized backpack that was large enough for the suit as well as his schoolwork.

"We need you to keep this with you at all times. The suit is made of a material that is virtually indestructible. Please wear it whenever you're required to expose your unique abilities in public. This will keep your identity private."

"No worries," Zax grinned. *I love this job!* he thought.

30

The weekend passed slowly as Zax waited for the results of his history exam. Finally, the day arrived. One at a time, students were being called up to see their results. Some of them smiled while others silently cried on the way back to their seats.

"Zax," Ms. Matthews called.

Zax rose from his desk and nervously walked to the front of the room. He'd been confident he had passed with flying colors, but when Emily Rose—one of the smartest kids in school—cried on her way back to her desk, he started to become worried.

At first glance, he saw nothing but zeros and fifteens on the grade sheet. Then he got to his name. He skimmed over to his score with his heart pounding like a jackhammer. He passed. And with seventy-five percent. He grinned from ear to ear as he walked back to his desk.

After class, he found out that Jaiden and a few other people had passed as well. Even Jack had passed. Obviously, he wasn't the only one who had studied hard. Everyone except Jaiden seemed angry about him passing, but he didn't really care. They already hated him anyway.

Zax headed back home and thought how nice it was that he didn't have to run into the woods every day just to get there. He plowed through the door and told Jenny and Ethan that he passed. They were thrilled.

"Great job! Now you can go on the field trip, right?" Jenny asked.

"If Agent Morrison can convince the director, that is. Since the fight with the Chupacabra, he has not given any orders," Ethan said.

"Oh yeah, I forgot to tell you, the director needs me to check out this energy thing at the beach in San Diego. Agent Morrison told me about it and said they would pay my expenses."

Zax could see the fury in Ethan's eyes for being kept out of the loop.

Wonder if I should tell him about the suit? Zax thought. *Nah.*

The Brute

31

It was Saturday morning—the day of their departure. Zax had to get up earlier than everyone else going on the field trip in order to stop by the office. He had started calling the "agency" the "office" since it was housed in an office building. He thought it sounded better than saying agency all the time. It seemed logical.

Zax, Jenny, and Ethan arrived at the office to talk about the operation and what to look for when Zax got to San Diego. Apparently, Director Alvin had established a temporary office in an abandoned building near the ocean. This building had previously been their main headquarters, and they were now using it to monitor the waves. The address was 6623 Allen Road and was within walking distance of the hotel district. A three-minute walk, to be exact.

"Be on the watch for storm clouds. We think they form right before the waves. At least, that's what happened before," Agent Morrison said.

"Storm clouds? Ok. So, I'll be on the lookout for rain and really big waves," Zax said a bit sarcastically.

"This is really serious, Zax. You need to be on the lookout for some extremely large storm clouds. This is very unusual for San Diego."

"I know, I know. I'm on it," Zax said, changing his tone.

As Zax stood to leave, Agent Morrison opened his desk drawer, pulled out a cell phone, and held it in Zax's direction. "Go ahead," he said at Zax's hesitation. "Our team of engineers made this phone, especially for you, with your powers in mind. It's one of a kind, so whatever you do, take care of it."

Zax looked at Ethan and Jenny. They nodded their approval, and he took the phone from Agent Morrison's hand.

"I promise," he smiled.

32

The students and chaperones met up at Seattle-Tacoma International Airport for their 11:15 am nonstop departure to San Diego. Zax looked at his wristwatch as he wheeled his suitcase towards security. *About four hours until I'm on the beach,* he thought.

As he neared the security checkpoint, he saw Jaiden talking to someone he didn't know.

She saw him and waved. "Hey, Zax!" she said.

"Hey, Jaiden," he said as his bag rolled to a stop. "Who's this?"

"Oh, this is Mark. He and I went to the same school in Indiana. Our parents work together, so they had to move like we did," Jaiden said.

"Hi," Mark said and extended his hand. "It's nice to meet you."

"Nice to meet you too," Zax said as he took Mark's hand and squeezed as hard as he could. Now he remembered seeing him in their history class.

"That's a nice grip you got there," Mark said and squeezed back just as hard.

"Thanks. Yours isn't too bad either."

Jaiden could see the competition rising between Zax and Mark as neither let their grip subside. She tapped the top of their hands, trying to stop them from completely crushing each other. Their hands parted, and she said, "So now that you two have met, let's go to the beach and have some fun!" She turned and got in the security line with Zax and Mark following.

Within the hour, boarding began on their Southwest flight. With no pre-assigned seating, the competition between Mark and Zax re-emerged, and they fought by pushing each other out of the way for the seat next to Jaiden. In the end, they both lost. She ended up sitting next to another friend, and they ended up together. *At least her friend is a girl*, Zax thought.

Zax and Mark sat without saying a word for the first half-hour of the flight. Finally, Zax broke the silence by trying to make conversation. "So, how long have you known Jaiden?"

"Pretty much our entire life. We were childhood friends. What about you?" Mark said, fidgeting in his seat. He'd drawn the short straw and ended up in the middle.

"Only a few weeks," Zax said.

"Really?" Mark looked stunned. "I wouldn't think that she'd become friends with someone that fast again. You must be very special to her."

"What do you mean 'again'?"

"Well, the last time she became friends with someone that fast, they did something awful to her," he said.

"Like what?" Zax asked inquisitively.

"I shouldn't tell you. I've already told you too much," Mark said with regret on his face.

Zax turned around and saw Jaiden staring at Mark with a "you better sleep with one eye open" kind of look. Once Zax saw her face, he decided that maybe it was time to change the subject.

33

After the plane landed and everyone had their luggage, the group was shuttled to their hotel by bus. The hotel was adjacent to the beach, as was pretty much everything else—houses, stores, restaurants, and stuff like that. On the ride over, they were informed that their school group would occupy most of the second floor of the four-story building.

As they pulled up to the hotel, Zax and the other kids couldn't believe this was where they'd be staying. It looked atrocious. Snickers and outright laughter could be heard all around the bus at the sight of the dark green walls framed in orange.

"Who thought green and orange were a good color combo?" someone whispered.

"How was this approved?" someone else mumbled. "If this is what it looks like outside, can you imagine the inside?"

"What do you two think?" Zax asked Mark and Jaiden, laughing.

"I think it's an abomination. How did anyone think this was a good idea," Mark said, shaking his head.

"I think it's interesting and unique," Jaiden said trying to be diplomatic.

"I think they were color blind and thought the colors were something else," Zax said.

"Ha-ha, maybe," she said.

Zax, Mark, and Jaiden followed their classmates inside and grabbed their room keys. Mark and Zax looked at each other's keys and realized they were sharing a room. The question now was, who was their third roommate? They had been told there would be three to a room, but no one knew who was sharing with who until check-in. The only other thing they had been told was that the girls were on one side of the hallway, the boys on the other. Why the teachers kept it a secret was anyone's guess. Zax, unlike the others, had no idea why it was a big deal.

Zax and Mark opened the door to their room, Room 214, having already discussed a plan to unpack and head straight to the beach. They stepped inside to see there were three twin beds, a chair, a desk with a light above it, and a tiny bathroom. Someone was standing next to the bed on the far side of the room— the unknown roommate.

In the dimly lit room, Zax couldn't tell who it was. Then the shadowy figure looked up. It was Jack. *Great*, Zax thought. *I'm going to die in my sleep. I can see the news headline now, "Kid Strangled in His Sleep, Suspect Not Found." I must be in the wrong room. That's it. I'll just apologize and leave and tell the teacher there was a mistake.*

"Hey Jack, is this your room?" Zax asked,

glancing down at his keycard. "Sorry. I must be in the wrong room."

"No, you're not. You two are my roommates. I caught a peek at the room arrangements when the teacher wasn't looking on the bus," Jack said.

"Who are you?" Mark asked.

"This is Jack from school. He is a bull…"

"I *was* a bully, at least to you," Jack interrupted. "But I saw what you did to that monster, and I know that whatever you did to it, you did to my arm and healed it. I don't know what you are or how you do it, but you have my word that I'll never bully you again. And, if I can, I'll stop bullying others too."

Jack paused and briefly looked at the floor before returning his gaze to Zax. "Thanks, Zax. You're a good guy, and you never deserved to be treated the way I treated you. I'm really sorry."

Zax was shocked and speechless. *Is this really Jack?* he wondered.

Mark looked at Zax then at Jack. It was obvious that he was puzzled by the conversation. "My name is Mark," he said, extending his hand to Jack.

Mark's hand brushed past Zax's shoulder and snapped him out of the shock-induced trance brought on by Jack's statement. *Crap*, Zax thought. *I forgot Mark was here. I'm sure he heard about the Chupacabra, but virtually no one except Jack and Jaiden knows that I was the one who killed it or that I helped heal Jack's arm. And that's the way I want it to stay.*

Zax looked at Jack who had the same "Oh crap" look on his face. He knew they were probably thinking the same thing.

Jack immediately realized he needed to say something. He *had* to say something. He reached for Mark's hand and hoped that whatever explanation he was about to give was believable.

"I'm Jack," he said, lightly gripping Mark's hand and releasing it quickly. "About that monster thing I mentioned…when I was in middle school, some kid drew a picture of me that was very offensive and rude. I called it a monster and punched the person who drew it. He, in return, punched my arm—and it hurt like hell—but Zax took the drawing and ripped it up. It made me feel better, and…it healed my arm, metaphorically speaking."

"Oh, ok. I guess that makes sense. Whatever," Mark said. He tossed his bag on the bed and began unpacking. Zax and Jack looked at each other as if they'd just dodged a bullet and began unpacking, as well.

After emptying his suitcase, Mark left to meet up with another friend. Zax and Jack took a long sigh of relief and fell on their beds.

"Good job with that story," Zax said, staring at the ceiling. "Where did it come from?"

"Part of it was true. Part of it wasn't," Jack said.

"What does that mean?"

"What it sounds like. In middle school, someone drew a very offensive drawing of me, and I got mad. But I didn't punch anyone. It really pissed me off, though, but I just sat there. Then someone I didn't know went up to the kid and said, 'Why would you do this? This is crossing the line.' He ripped up the drawing and punched the person who drew it," Jack said. "I didn't pay much attention at the time, but after seeing you fight that monster, I realized it was you who stood up for me. The look in your eye—your pissed-off look—was the same look that kid had in his eye. That's another reason why I'm not going to bully you anymore."

"I never knew. I'm sorry, I forgot."

"It's ok. I don't know why you're apologizing to me. You've helped me twice, and all I've done is bully you. *I* should be apologizing," he said, looking at his healed arm.

"Others will still do it, and if you try to help, you'll probably be bullied too," Zax said, still looking up.

"Do you think I care if anyone bullies me? Maybe if I intervene, they'll stop," he said. "And, by the way, I'm really struggling to explain how my arm healed so quickly."

Zax's phone buzzed. It was a message from Jaiden. "At the beach. Come over. See you soon."

"We'll talk about this later," Zax said and headed out the door.

"Ok. See you later."

34

By the time Zax got to the beach, Jaiden and Mark and some other kids were in the water splashing each other.

"Hey, Jaiden, Mark. I'm here," Zax shouted and wondered if they could hear him over the waves.

"Hey, you're late," Jaiden yelled. "Mark got here before you. I thought you were faster than him with your power and all."

Zax started to freak out again. He knew there was no way that Mark hadn't just heard what she blurted out. Jaiden laughed jokingly.

Mark saw the 'how could you' look on Zax's face, then turned to Jaiden. "So, I'm guessing you haven't told Zax that you told me?" he asked.

"What do you mean? Told you what?" Zax quizzed angrily, clutching his backpack.

"She told me about the energy and pretty much everything."

Zax looked at Jaiden, disappointed. "Why would you do that?" he asked. "And is it really that funny?"

Jaiden stopped laughing and lowered her head. "I'm so sorry, Zax," she said as tears began to form in her eyes. "There's nothing funny about it. I swear I thought you had already told Mark about your power."

Zax took a deep breath contemplating what to say. He didn't want to say something he would regret.

Just as he was about to speak, a loud boom of thunder echoed across the beach, and a huge, ominous, black cloud began forming offshore in the distance.

"I have to go," Zax said anxiously. Running back away from the ocean, he yelled, "Mark, I need you and Jaiden and all the other kids to get back to the hotel. There's a bad storm coming. This might have something to do with that monster at school."

"Are you staying? Do you need help?" Jaiden yelled as Zax continued running away.

"I'm good. Just go. I don't want you two to get hurt."

"But what if *you* get hurt?" she pleaded.

"I won't get hurt; I promise. Now go! And tell the lifeguards to clear the beach. I think something bad is about to happen."

Mark grabbed Jaiden's arm and raced her back to the hotel. They ran to the rooftop deck so they could watch what was going on. When they got there, they found Jack standing against the railing. He said he'd heard the thunder and decided to check the weather out before slathering on sunscreen and heading to the beach. There was nothing worse than putting on sunscreen to simply have to take it off.

35

Zax ran into a restroom building, pulled his suit from his backpack, and quickly put it on. As soon as he made it back to the ocean's edge, clouds started swirling above him. From out of nowhere, a giant wave rose slowly and barreled in his direction. The beach was lined with a large continuous mound of sand—a dune—designed and constructed to protect the oceanfront buildings from flooding. Before Zax could take any action, the wave pushed him backwards into the dune. Once the first wave went away, another even bigger one hit him. Then another, and another. Zax knew that if he didn't do something quickly, these waves would destroy the dune and flood the city. Finally, he caught a break and made a bubble of the energy so he wouldn't feel the full force of the waves. The bubble still had some rough edges; he needed more practice.

But even with the energy bubble, the waves were still strong enough to push him back. After a few minutes of punching waves, Zax was able to mitigate the effect of the waves by turning the bubble into a solid wall up and down the beach that drove the old waves back into the new ones. The giant waves stopped coming, but something else, something even more sinister, appeared. A giant monster slowly emerged from the ocean. As it approached, it became obvious that its heavy footsteps and body motion were what had caused the enormous waves.

The giant monster looked something like a gorilla, except it was about fifty feet tall, had red skin, three eyes on its chest, no neck or head, and wore tan pants, for some reason. No shirt. No shoes.

What the…? Zax thought. *Tan pants?* He knew, however, he could not be distracted by the pants on this gigantic monster in front of him.

He made an energy spear and threw it at the monster, but this time, there was a tether of energy that connected his wrist to the spear. The beast caught the spear and pulled Zax upward towards him. He knew he was going to need a different weapon, something sharp and strong that had a closer range for battle.

The energy swirled around his hand, and it felt the same as the spear, but even stronger. It started to stretch out and grew twig-like streams of energy before forming a sword in his hand.

As Zax swung close to the beast, he stabbed it in the shoulder with the sword. The beast threw the spear that was still connected to Zax. The tether pulled him with the spear, and he ended up cutting clean through the beast's shoulder with an upward slash.

Zax fell to the ground and immediately ran back towards the beast. Once he made it, he saw the beast grabbing its shoulder from the pain of the cut. The beast tried to punch down at Zax, but Zax jumped out of the way of the large fist that raced towards him. He quickly leaped onto the beast's arm and scrambled up, trying for a chest hit. But before he could make it to the top of its arm, the beast tried slapping him with its other hand.

Zax jumped away from the beast. Though it was the opposite way he wanted to go, he made a backwards swipe at the beast's arm as he jumped. To his surprise, a massive wave of energy, traveling at high speed, came off the sword and cut the beast in half. Just like the Chupacabra, the beast screamed, then evaporated into a purple dust. Almost instantaneously, the waves disappeared, and the storm clouds began to dissipate.

36

Zax quickly ran back to the restroom, changed, and secured his suit in his backpack, then sprinted to the hotel to check on Jaiden, Mark, and Jack.

When Zax opened the door to the lobby, all three of them rushed towards him.

"What happened? Are you ok?" Jaiden asked. "Was that you in the superhero's suit?"

"Yes, it was me, but we must all keep that as our secret. I'm ok. A bit waterlogged, but ok," Zax answered.

"Where did that sword come from?" Jack asked.

"Yeah. Where did that come from? I haven't seen that before," Jaiden said.

"To tell the truth, I have no idea," Zax replied.

"You really do have powers," Mark said in disbelief. "How do you have powers? Where did those weapons come from? And what was that thing?"

"I don't know how I have powers, but the weapons came from the strange energy I control," Zax paused. "As for that thing, I have no idea. This is the second time something like this has happened and, thinking back, it all started after our run-in with Professor Brian."

"One thing is for sure," Jack said, "You definitely know how to use the weapons. How did you learn so fast?"

"To tell the truth, again, I have no idea. When I touched Jaiden's phone, visions of fighting monsters like that flooded my head. It seemed like I'd received years of fighting experience in a flash. Or it could be that I'm just a really fast learner," he smiled.

"So, now what?" Mark asked.

"I need to go check on someone. I'll be back in an hour or two," Zax said.

Jaiden, Mark, and Jack looked at each other, mystified, then agreed they would keep Zax's secret between them.

37

Zax considered making another energy board but decided the walk to the office on Allen Road would do him good. Besides, he was curious to see just how accurate Agent Morrison had been at quoting the three-minute trek. He glanced at his watch to time the walk, and precisely three minutes later, he was standing in front of 6623 Allen Road.

This can't be right. They must have given me the wrong address, he thought staring at the decrepit building.

The rundown, one-story building bearing that address had broken windows and walls that were falling apart. He double-checked the note app on his phone, and, sure enough, the address was the same. That's when he noticed the logo on the building's only door. The yellow globe with ripples emitting from it was unmistakable. It was the same logo that was on the front door of their other building. He was in the right place.

He walked to the door and knocked, and without warning, the welcome mat below him sprung open, and he fell into something akin to a slide, with crazy twists and turns. Zax landed in a room that looked identical to the one with the hologram table back at the office. Agent Morrison was sitting in the room and looked as though he was about to cry with laughter. Zax stood up, trying to figure out what Agent Morrison found so funny. Then he turned and saw the monitor behind him. It was replaying him going down the slide, freaking out.

"You'd better delete that," Zax sneered.

"It's a bit too late for that," Agent Morrison chuckled.

"What does that mean?" Zax said, failing to see any humor.

"It means that this video is being streamed to the office as we speak," he said with a stupid smile on his face.

"Whatever," Zax said. "Wait, I'm not the only person that calls the agency the 'office'?"

"Nope. We all call it the office. Why do you think we always use office buildings as our workplace?" he asked.

"I don't know. I thought it was kind of strange, but..." Zax said. "Anyway, that's not the point. Did you see what I did? I killed that Brute thing. Did this resolve the energy issue we saw in the hologram?"

"I know you killed it. I saw you. I was watching from the roof of an adjacent building," Agent Morrison said and folded his arms on the table. "And, yes, everything is back to normal. You can go and have fun until you return home."

"So, no party? No celebration? No nothing? I risked my life! Actually, I've risked it *several* times!"

"Good job. How about that?" Agent Morrison replied smugly.

"Guess that will have to do," Zax snapped. *Unbelievable. You're welcome, by the way!* he thought. "See you next week at home," he added as he turned to leave.

Zax heard a thump and turned back. A tube popped out of the hologram table with a letter from the director.

Agent Morrison retrieved the letter and read it to himself, then looked up at Zax. "Seems as though you're going to have to report back here tomorrow for some specialized training," he said holding the letter.

"What happened to having fun?"

"You will, but only when you're finished training. Sorry," he said, "I just got these orders."

Zax sighed. *So much for the beach*, he thought.

"Well, I guess I'll see you tomorrow then," Zax said as he started to leave again. "Wait. How do I get out of here?"

Agent Morrison smiled and pointed to a wall switch. "That will lead you upstairs to the back door."

Zax walked over and flipped the switch. A section of the wall moved sideways revealing a hidden staircase. He glanced back at Agent Morrison with a "you gotta be kidding me" look, then climbed the stairs and left.

When Zax got back to the hotel, he told Jaiden, Mark, and Jack about the meeting at the office. He explained that he had to go in for training the following day and that he needed them to cover for him. They were all in.

The Storm

38

The next day, the day after he fought the Brute, Zax got up early and snuck out of the hotel. Jack and Mark told the chaperones he wasn't feeling well and needed to rest. They bought it.

When he got to the San Diego office, Zax started the same training that he had done with Ethan and Jenny. This time, however, the scenarios in the holograms were harder and, with the gun lessons, the targets were smaller. Everything was more difficult, and every session lasted longer.

"How long before we're done with this?" Zax asked.

"Soon. We just need to do one more test," Agent Morrison replied.

"Ok, what is it?"

"We're going to take off your training wheels."

"What does that mean?"

"Exactly what it sounds like. I'm going to put you in a room, and I want you to let loose. Go all out. Release all the energy you can," he said while shuffling a stack of papers.

"I thought your job was to make sure I *didn't* lose control. Won't I lose control if I release too much energy?" Zax asked, confused.

"The room you will be in is practically indestructible. It's stronger than a nuke shelter."

Zax wasn't sure how he felt about this, but it seemed he really didn't have a choice.

Agent Morrison put Zax in an underground room that he hadn't seen before. The room was pitch dark and reeked with the awful, putrid smell of rotten eggs. He closed the door behind him, shutting Zax inside. For a few minutes, Zax contemplated what he was about to do. Then he closed his eyes and unleashed all his power with a giant explosion. The explosion was much like the one back at his old house when he fought the SWAT agents. Zax immediately felt like he was about to pass out.

"Good. Now do it again and don't pass out," Agent Morrison said over the intercom.

"What? I'm surprised I didn't pass out this time!"

"Better not because the boss hasn't taken the reward off your head. I could kill you while you're out and pocket a big reward. A memo went out to all the agents yesterday stating that we still had the ok to take you out if we felt you were getting out of control. Bet you didn't know anything about that, did you?"

Though he couldn't see Agent Morrison's face, Zax could hear the smugness in his voice. *That's it*, Zax thought. Now he was *really* angry.

Zax built up every ounce of his remaining power and released it all at once, saving just enough to keep him awake. The room was destroyed, and the building almost collapsed. Zax opened his eyes and saw Agent Morrison's face—stunned and terrified—by what had just happened. The walls of the room were in piles of rubble around him. This energy blast felt different. It seemed stronger and more powerful than ever before.

"Ok, you pass," Agent Morrison said, gazing at the destruction. "This was all just a test. Oh, and that threat I made? It was just a joke. I wouldn't try to kill you."

Though Zax heard what Agent Morrison said about not killing him, the look in his eyes told Zax that maybe it wasn't a joke.

"Whatever. I don't care. But it's good to know that people are still authorized to try and kill me, at least," Zax said. He stepped over the fallen debris and left.

39

Zax took the elevator to his room once he got back to the hotel. He was too exhausted for stairs. When he walked in, Mark and Jack were on their phones. Jack was on the bed, and Mark was sitting in the chair. They glanced at each other after seeing the look on Zax's face, which seemed to say he could kill everything and everyone in the building. But they both knew better. Zax would never hurt an innocent person.

"Hey," Zax said before falling onto his bed and closing his eyes. He was not in the mood for conversation.

"You ok?" Jack asked.

Not now, Zax thought. "Yeah, just tired."

"You sure? It looks like you've had the life sucked out of you," Mark said.

Zax tried to remain cool. He rolled over, and with his back to his roommates, he said, "I'm good. Just tired and need to sleep for a while."

40

Zax was in a dark room again, like the one at his new house and at Jaiden's. The energy light was there, but this time it was very small. Candle-size small. The energy used to look like a spotlight in his face. Now it was simply a tiny flame.

"Are you ok?" Zax asked the energy.

"The question is, are *you* ok?" the energy asked.

"What do you mean?"

"I mean that you need to get the energy that you lost back. I will give you the rest of me, but you will need to get all that you lost before I go out," it said.

"Wait, the energy that I lost? What do you mean by that?" Zax asked anxiously.

"I don't have time to explain. You will find out once you get the energy back."

"How do I do that? How do I get the energy back?" he asked.

"You will know when it tries coming back to you."

The energy light rushed towards him, and Zax felt as if he had just been struck by lightning. He was jolted to consciousness and realized he was sitting next to Jack on the plane.

41

"Where are we?" Zax asked, both startled and confused. "How did I get here?"

Jack looked at him as though he'd lost his mind. "We're flying home," he said. "And you got here the same way we all did."

Zax looked around the plane. "Last thing I remember is falling asleep on the bed back at the hotel," he said, holding his chest.

"You were saying weird things while we were boarding, like 'need power back' and 'you will know when it tries coming back to you.' That type of stuff," Jack said.

"That's what happened in my dream," Zax mumbled.

"That's really weird," Jack said under his breath and turned to look out the plane's window.

Zax wondered how he was supposed to reconnect to the energy. He was left with more questions—different questions—and no answers. *When I get home, I've got to figure this out,* he thought.

As the flight reached its cruising altitude, it was unexpectedly thrust into an unpredicted thunderstorm with violent turbulence.

The pilot's voice came over the speaker. "Ladies and gentlemen, please remain calm. We're passing through an unexpected storm, but everything will be fine. Please stay in your seats with your seatbelts fastened."

Zax peered over Jack and looked out the window. A frightening thought suddenly occurred to him. Maybe the Brute wasn't actually dead. If he wasn't, he might be the cause of this storm. With modern technology, a storm of this magnitude would have been flagged, and this plane would *not* have taken off. *If that's the case, this plane is going to crash,* he thought. Before Zax could come up with a plan, a streak of lightning flew directly past his window. The noise was deafening.

The lightning and rain were intense, and Zax got a weird feeling in his stomach. It felt like the energy, but he didn't see it anywhere. There were no yellow swirls like he normally saw or the flow it had whenever he controlled it. *So why am I having this feeling?* he wondered.

He looked out the window and saw the lightning. Then it hit him. The lightning *was* the energy. It was concentrating into a powerful bolt and was out of control. And it was focused on him.

The situation continued to get worse. The lightning repeatedly struck the plane where Zax was sitting, rocking it back and forth. The plane had stopped losing altitude, but everyone was still freaking out. He knew he had to do something—but what? The plane could only take so much punishment.

He couldn't just walk out of the plane. Not only would everyone see him, but he didn't feel like his chances of surviving the fall were very good.

At that moment, the door went flying off the hinges and was swept away. With that, Zax realized he was going to end up outside the plane one way or another. He unbuckled his seatbelt and rushed to the opening. It was the only way to save the other lives on this plane.

"What do you think you're doing?" Jaiden screamed.

"To be honest, I don't know," he yelled.

Zax looked at her, waved his hand, and jumped.

The wind blew into his face as he fell towards the rocky mountain. Lightning bolts flew all around him. He looked up and saw a huge gathering of light in the clouds, then a giant streak of lightning started rushing right at him—the biggest he had seen yet. The massive bolt of energy struck him directly. Though it would have literally fried anyone else, it had no effect on him. As the energy entered his body, it felt warm and pleasant, not hot and painful. Instantly, everything went dark again.

42

Zax woke up in his room with his posters, desk, and all his stuff, down to the wrinkle on his bed. He started to walk out of his room until he noticed that there was nothing but darkness when he opened his door. He thought that maybe he had passed out, hit the ground, and died on impact. He turned around to see a perfect reflection of himself, though there was no mirror. He pinched himself to make sure that this wasn't a dream. He didn't feel anything from the pinch, so he guessed that he was dreaming again. Or that he was dead.

"No, you're not dead," the other Zax, the reflection, said.

"Who are you? Have I met you other than when I look in the mirror, I mean?" Zax asked.

"Yes, we've already met," the reflection said. "At your friend's house, at your house, and at the hotel."

"You're the energy! I've never seen you take a form before. I've only seen you as a really bright light. What's different this time?"

"You are full of energy, unlike before."

"So, I was right. The lightning *was* the energy," Zax said.

"Yes. When you use the energy, do you ever wonder where it goes?"

"No, I just thought it went back into the ground and back to the core."

"Yes and no," his reflection explained. "When you use the energy, it evaporates into the air and travels with thunderstorm clouds then zaps back into the earth. What people think is lightning is, in actuality, concentrated and uncontrolled energy trying to get back into the earth."

"Like the water cycle?"

"Yes, something like that. When you're active, you begin to deplete the energy you receive from the earth's core. Over time, this energy will be naturally replenished. However, it may take days, if not a week, for your energy level to fully replenish. When you are subjected to lightning, you short circuit the process and quickly replenish your supply. When you jumped out of the plane, you were struck numerous times by the concentrated energy—plus a giant bolt of pure energy—just before you passed out. As a result, the energy you depleted at the office in San Diego has been fully restored. You are now at max energy and ready for action."

"Then why am I here and not back on the plane or wherever I'm supposed to be?"

"So that I can tell you to go back to your old house in the woods to find the final beast. He is the one who will lead you to the source of all three beasts.

This won't happen for a few months, so go and have fun with your friends until then. And train like your life depends on it. Because it does."

"So, what's this beast's name?" Zax asked.

"Dark Matter, D.M. for short. You will know why once you meet it. I'm running out of time. Go and get ready."

With that, Zax woke up in his bedroom. Jaiden, Mark, Jack, Jenny, and Ethan were hovering above him.

"He's awake!" Ethan shouted as Zax slowly opened his eyes.

"What were you thinking?" Jaiden asked hysterically. "You could've died!"

"What happened? Am I at home? How did you find me?" Zax asked weakly. He looked around the room and tried to figure out what was going on.

"You walked out of the plane, got hit by a giant bolt of lightning, and fell on the snowy summit of a mountain," Mark said.

"And luckily, the snow was soft enough to break your fall along with the shield of energy you had created around yourself," Jack added.

"A hiker found you and took you to his cabin. He warmed you up and called the police. We identified you using the office's tracking devices, and we brought you back home," Ethan explained.

"What happened to the plane? Is everyone ok?"

"With a cabin door missing, the pilot somehow landed it in the ocean not too far from the shore of northern Oregon. Crews were quickly on site after it landed and made sure everyone was safe and accounted for," Jaiden said taking his hand. "The strange thing is that the storm disappeared right after you jumped out of the plane."

"You've been out almost two weeks," Jack said. "It's Saturday. The three of us just happened to stop by this morning to check on your condition. Glad to see you finally awake."

"So, really, why did you jump out of the plane?" Mark asked.

Zax thought the lightning should be a secret— just in case—so they wouldn't worry about him.

"I tend to sleepwalk from time to time. Guess I fell asleep right before the storm," Zax said. He knew they didn't believe it, not even for a second.

He saw concern in their eyes and heard worry in their voices as they simply said, "Ok, sure," then left him to rest. He didn't know what this Dark Matter thing was, but what he *did* know was that he didn't want anyone to get hurt, like they could have, had he not jumped from the plane.

"I need to run away," he whispered to himself.

Returning Home

43

When Zax got to school the following Monday, he found everything to be the same, except that fewer people were making fun of him. Jack had spread the word that he and Zax were friends. That all but eliminated the bullying.

As the days flew by, he continued his training, spent as much time with Jaiden as he could, and started thinking about a plan to get away and challenge the D.M. without involving his family or friends. He simply could not tell Jenny and Ethan that he was returning to the old house to fight another monster.

On Friday morning, several weeks later, Zax grabbed his backpack and headed downstairs. This was the day. He would put his plan into action after school.

He walked into the kitchen where Jenny and Ethan were having their morning cup of coffee.

"Hey, I'm not going to need a ride this afternoon," he said standing in the doorway. "I joined a club that meets after school today, and, if it's ok, I'm going to spend the night at Mark's house." He knew they wouldn't care if he stayed at Mark's, but he thought the right thing to do was ask. Less suspicion that way.

"Ok with me," Ethan said.

"Are you sure? We can pick you up after the meeting and bring you to Mark's later," Jenny said.

"I'm sure. We already made plans. I assumed you would be ok with it," Zax said smiling.

"Of course, we are," Jenny said. "Ready to go?"

Zax nodded and said, "See you tomorrow, Ethan." As he walked to the car and waited for Jenny to take him to school, he couldn't help but think that that was way easier than expected.

44

When the final school bell rang, Zax hurriedly found Mark and told him everything about his plan. He wasn't worried about telling Mark because he had complete confidence in their friendship, and that's what he needed at the moment—someone he could trust explicitly. Though he could completely trust Jaiden and Jack, he didn't want them to know. He really didn't want Mark to know either, but he had no choice since he told Jenny and Ethan he was staying at his house.

Zax was heading for the front door when Jaiden saw him from afar in the hall. As planned, Mark ran and bumped into her. Her books went flying everywhere.

"Oh, I'm sorry," Mark said, playing the part perfectly.

"It's ok," Jaiden said. "It was my fault for not watching where I was going."

"Let me help you pick your things up. Looks like you're trying to get somewhere quick," Mark said.

By the time Jaiden looked back up, Zax was gone.

45

Zax was running through the parking lot, filled only with the sounds of kids thrilled to be out of school, when he heard, "Hey, I'm going with you."

He turned around and saw Jack.

"Go with me where? What do you mean?" Zax asked, stopping for a moment.

"I mean, I'm going with you to help you fight this thing," Jack said.

"No, you're not. That's final!"

"You're gonna need some help. I understand why you don't want anyone else to go, but you need at least one person, and who better than a quarterback?"

Zax knew he wouldn't be able to convince Jack not to come. The look in Jack's eyes was recognizable. He'd seen it before in Ethan's, in Jenny's, in Jaiden's, and in his own. The look you have when you won't stop until you know that someone you care about is safe.

"Wait, how did you even know that I was doing this?"

"I heard you tell your plan to Mark while we were in the hall."

"Guess I wasn't very discreet when I told him," Zax mumbled with aggravation at himself.

"Yeah, you need to be more careful. What if it was Jaiden who heard and not me?"

"Why were you eavesdropping?"

"I was on my way to the door, and I heard 'distract Jaiden.' I was trying to make sure you weren't going to prank her or something."

"Why would I, of all people, try to prank her?"

"Because friends prank each other. Unless…" Jack paused and grinned, "you want to be more than friends with her."

"No! It's nothing like that!" Zax said, blushing. He turned back around and started running again. "Are you coming with me or what?"

46

They got to the edge of the woods and were heading for the house when Zax heard a rustling noise coming from the trees. He stopped.

"You ok?" asked Jack.

"Yeah. I thought I heard something."

"I didn't hear anything."

"It must have been the wind in the trees, I guess," Zax shrugged.

They took a few more steps, then Zax felt a heavy weight fall upon him, like forced pressure. *Could this be because of the D.M.? If it is, it's extremely strong,* he thought.

"Are you sure you're ok?" Jack said seeing Zax stumble.

"I don't know. It feels like a hundred pounds was just dropped on top of me."

"Can you move?"

"Yeah, but it feels like I'm about to fall over."

Their pace slowed a bit, but they kept going until they arrived at the house. It looked exactly the same as it did the last time Zax was there, except the vehicles had been removed from the lake. The office had a team of mechanics who could take any vehicle and make it new again. This certainly wasn't his home anymore. As much as Zax hated the place, some good memories had been made there. Like when the spider landed on Ethan, and he freaked out. Or when Jenny taught him to cook. He'd had fun there too.

Once they got into the house, he and Jack decided to split up to cover more ground. Jack agreed to take the downstairs, Zax the upstairs.

As Zax neared the top step, he heard a loud crash coming from his old room. He rushed inside to see what was going on. Standing there in front of him was an unworldly, humanoid looking thing. But it definitely wasn't human. It had large eyes with the smallest pupils he'd ever seen and had wings for its arms. Both wings had three claws coming off of them. The second it saw Zax, it turned into the same purple dust that the Chupacabra and Brute did when they had died.

The dust swirled around the room, then regrouped and flew outside through a cracked window—the window closest to where his bed used to be.

"What was that? I heard a crash," Jack yelled as he pounded up the stairs.

"I think it was the reason we came here," Zax said.

"The D.M. thing?"

"Yeah," he said and quickly darted past Jack.

Jack followed Zax outside, though he did not know what was going on or what they were looking for. Zax looked around. The D.M. was nowhere to be seen, yet somehow, he sensed it was nearby.

"Stay by the house, Jack!" Zax demanded. No sooner than the warning came out of his mouth, the D.M. swooped in from nowhere for an attack. Jack ducked and hunkered down by the front steps.

Zax hurriedly made a sword from the energy, like the one he made in the battle with the Brute, and used it to block the strike. He tried going for a swing, but the D.M. grabbed the blade with its talons. Zax managed to pull the sword away, get rid of it, and take out a spear, also made from the energy. He threw it at the D.M., but the D.M. flew up and dodged it.

Zax knew he needed a new weapon. The sword was usless, and the D.M. was faster than the spear. The energy started spiraling around his hand as if it were creating another sword or spear. Then it transformed into something completely different. It had the length of a spear, but at the end, something grew that looked like half of a crescent moon. It had formed into a scythe.

Zax swung at the beast. It tried dodging the weapon, but the scythe caught it on the edge of its right wing. The D.M. made a high-pitched screeching noise, freaked out, and flew off. Zax was momentarily stunned by the high-pitched noise and fell to the ground. *This beast cannot win*, he thought.

He scrambled to his feet and swung the scythe again as the beast circled. This time, he hit the beast in the back.

He thought the scythe went through the beast, but as he looked closer, he realized it hadn't. He wasn't as close to the D.M. as he'd thought. The beast flew up and away and disappeared over the forest. It did not come back. It was the first beast that had gotten away.

Zax ran back to Jack and grabbed his arm. "We need to go."

"Yeah," Jack said, visibly shaken. "What was that? Are you gonna tell your parents and Jaiden?"

"Ethan and Jenny, yeah. Jaiden? I'm not ready to die yet," Zax said as they ran from the house.

"You're probably right."

Once they got to Jack's house, Zax and Jack split up but not before Zax swore Jack to secrecy. Zax dreaded what he had to do next, but he knew he had to go home and fess up. Not only did he have to tell Ethan and Jenny he lied about staying at Mark's, now he had to tell them about the D.M.

"Ethan is going to be *so* mad about all of this," Zax said.

The Dark Matter

47

Ethan and Jenny were finishing a late dinner when Zax walked into the house and told them the whole story. They both seemed agitated with him.

"So, you didn't kill it?" Jenny asked with a frown on her face.

"Great," Ethan said, "Now it's mad, and most likely, it followed you!"

"You put your friend and us in danger!" Jenny said.

The room went silent for a moment. Ethan shook his head and said, "You need to go to your room. We need to prepare for a fight. You seem to be useless against this monster. I guess *we'll* have to kill it."

"Yeah. Just go to your room," Jenny agreed angrily.

"Um, ok. I'm exhausted anyway," Zax said and started towards his room. "By the way, I'm fine. Thanks for asking," he added.

"Just stay there if you're so tired. We'll tell you when it's dead!" Ethan yelled furiously.

Something wasn't right. Zax had expected Ethan to get mad; he always did. But Jenny, rarely ever.

The fight with the D.M. had depleted much of his energy. He was too tired to think about what was going on with Jenny. He went to his bedroom and fell on his bed. As soon as his head hit the pillow, he passed out.

48

When Zax woke up the next morning, he thought about last night and was totally confused. He couldn't help but think about how angry Ethan and Jenny had been the night before, especially Jenny. That was just not like her. *Whatever,* he thought. He rolled over, got up, and dressed for school.

Jenny and Ethan were sitting at the breakfast table with coffee and toast when he walked into the kitchen. Neither looked up or acknowledged him. He looked around and was surprised to see that Jenny did not have any food on the table other than what she and Ethan were eating. It was bizarre because she always had breakfast ready and waiting for him by the time he got downstairs. If nothing else, she had cereal. But there was nothing. Not even cereal. Something was definitely off.

"Where's my breakfast?" Zax asked. "I'm starving."

"Why don't you make your own food," Jenny snapped. "We work too, you know."

"Sorry. I was just hungry," Zax said as he popped two slices of bread in the toaster. It wasn't that he *couldn't* make his own breakfast; it was just weird that Jenny hadn't.

"You're lucky that the…whatever you called it didn't follow you back home," Ethan said, still obviously angry.

"I'm sorry about that too. I didn't know what else to do other than come home and tell you," Zax said.

"Who cares," Jenny snapped again. "And stop apologizing so much. It shows weakness. Get out of here and go to school, or you'll be late!"

Zax stared at Jenny, wondering what had invaded her body. Whatever it was, this Jenny was certainly not the Jenny he knew. He left the bread in the toaster, grabbed a banana, and took off.

When he got to school, no one said, "Hey Caveman" or "Did you get this new game?" or anything. Zax thought it was weird but assumed, once again, it was because of Jack. It was nice, but it was certainly weird.

His banana was long gone by lunchtime, and he was ready for lunch with Jaiden. He couldn't wait to tell her about his strange morning. They usually met in the hallway just outside the cafeteria, but she wasn't waiting when he got there. He looked around and saw her standing alone in the corner of the large room.

"Hey Jaiden," Zax said walking towards her.

"What? Are you going to act like nothing happened now?" she asked with disappointment in her eyes.

"What do you mean?" Zax asked, wondering what he could've possibly done.

"Wow," she said as her eyes began to water. "You can never accept that you do anything wrong, can you?"

Zax stood in shock and watched Jaiden run to her best friend, bawling. He would never hurt her. *Never.*

He glanced around the room again and saw Mark. *Maybe he knows what's going on,* Zax thought.

"Hey Mark, do you know what's wrong with Jaiden?" he asked.

"Um, do I know you?" Mark asked rudely. "Oh, wait, you're that kid who broke that girl's heart," he said pointing at Jaiden.

"What are you talking about? Break her heart? I haven't been dating her. Yet anyway."

"Well, you must have done something," he said. "What did you say your name was?"

"What's going on? You know who I am," Zax said, getting frustrated. "Do you know where Jack is?"

"Jack? I heard someone say he died a few weeks ago."

Ok, Zax thought. *What's going on here? Apparently, I've broken Jaiden's heart, and Mark doesn't know me. Oh yeah, and Jack died a few weeks ago even though I just saw him last night. Unless that was just a dream, and the plane DID crash into the mountain.*

Zax left the cafeteria and went to the bathroom to think; it was the quietest place in the school. He pushed the door open, and there stood the D.M.

When the D.M. saw Zax, it rushed into a bathroom stall. Zax went after it, shoving the stall door, only to find another student on his phone, staring at him. There was no D.M.

"I am *so* sorry; I didn't mean to barge in. You really should lock the door next time," Zax said, embarrassed, and pulled the stall door closed.

He left the bathroom confident that he'd seen the D.M. *Maybe my mind is playing tricks on me,* he thought. *But I need to investigate and figure out what is going on.*

Between classes, Zax went around school asking if anyone knew anything about him breaking Jaiden's heart or about Jack's death. It turned out that no one really knew if Jack was dead or not, but he was missing. As for Jaiden, she and Zax had supposedly started dating after the plane ride back home, and he had broken up with her the previous week over an argument. He also asked about the storm. Everyone he talked to looked at him as if he were crazy and said they knew nothing about a storm.

There is no way this is right. I know that storm happened! Unless I dreamed about that too. This is so strange.

Maybe someone back at the office will know something, he thought as he left campus for work that afternoon.

49

At the office, Zax used his passcode to enter the foyer, then stepped inside. To his surprise, there were no bullets whizzing toward him. There were no agents. The foyer was empty. He used his passcode again to pass through the security door and took an elevator to the fourth floor. *They must have been told to leave me alone*, he thought as he stepped off the elevator. Suddenly, every agent in the room shot out of their seats and tackled him. He tried knocking them off and pushing them away with outbursts of energy, but nothing worked; his powers seemed to be gone. With little effort, they secured him and escorted him to an interrogation room where Agent Morrison was waiting.

"So, who are you? How did you get into this building?" Agent Morrison asked.

"What are you talking about? I used my passcode," Zax replied.

"Your passcode? How did you get a passcode? The only way to get one is to be an agent here," he said, standing tall above Zax, who was seated in a chair.

"Wait a minute, there is something vaguely familiar about you," the director said to Zax as he entered the room.

"Sir, what do you mean by that?" Agent Morrison asked.

"Something isn't right here. I don't remember ever seeing this kid in my life, but I feel a great hatred toward him. How could I hate someone I don't even know?" the director asked.

"Well, what's the story, kid? You're in deep trouble, and you need to help us with some answers," Agent Morrison snapped.

Zax stared at the two men. It was as if Agent Morrison had taken on the director's harsh personality, and the director had mellowed to become more like Agent Morrison.

Zax told them everything about the energy, the beasts, the scans, all of it. They looked at him in disbelief. They were completely baffled. They claimed that they didn't have a scanner and knew nothing about this "energy" at the earth's core. But how, they asked, did he know so much about the agency? Finally, at Zax's insistence, the director decided to check their computer. After running a number of complex queries, they could find nothing about any scans or anything relative to Zax. As they were about to leave, Zax happened to notice a large file in the computer's recycle bin. For whatever reason, the file had not been deleted. Upon examination, the file confirmed that there actually *were* scans. The last scan generated was centered on the forest near his old house. It was dated one day ago. With this information, Zax was able to convince the director that the answer to this mystery must be in the forest. And, to clear up the matter, that's where he needed to go.

"Thank you for believing me," Zax said to the director.

"He might believe you, but I don't," said Agent Morrison.

"Just find out what's going on, and you won't need to thank me. By the way, my name is Alvin," the director said.

"Alvin?" Zax asked, surprised. He would have guessed Richard or William.

"Yes, do you have a problem with that?"

"No, sir," Zax said.

50

Zax immediately headed back to the forest near his old house to try and get answers. All at once, he heard a voice again. This time it sounded like Jack. *I must be losing my mind. I don't see him anywhere,* he thought.

As he came upon the house, he abruptly stopped. The lake was dried up. He heard Jack's voice again, only louder. Then, unexpectedly, he saw Jaiden, Mark, Ethan, and Jenny walking out of the woods.

"You're worthless," Jenny said.

"You've brought us nothing but pain," Ethan said.

"Just leave and never come back, freak," Mark said.

"We don't want you here," Jaiden said.

"We don't want you here," they repeated over and over in unison as they walked in Zax's direction, getting closer and closer together.

Once their bodies met, they merged into each other and began forming a single shape. Gradually it morphed into the D.M. It grew Ethan's face. "He doesn't want you here," the face said.

It grew Jenny's face. "She doesn't want you here."

It grew Mark's face. "He doesn't want you here."

It grew Jaiden's face. "And she doesn't want you here. So just go away into the abyss and stop trying to help people that don't want your help!"

Zax stood frozen for a moment before angrily confronting the D.M. "What have you done to my friends and family?"

"When you damaged my beautiful wing, I gave a high-pitched screech that hypnotized you. We are all inside your mind," the D.M. said, hovering above Zax. "None of this is real."

A whirlwind stirred, and Zax's energy materialized into a semi-transparent being identical to Zax. It scowled at the beast and said, "And for that reason, you're going to die today."

"What do you mean? I don't understand what is happening," Zax said to the energy without taking his eyes off the D.M.

"You have been traveling in an alternate reality while in an astral projection state. All your recent activities have been totally and completely in your head. The negative reaction to you by everyone you've encountered in this alternate reality was created by the D.M. to confuse, demoralize, and ultimately defeat you. But even so, you had the ability to manage the turmoil and return here with even more resolve to defeat the D.M.," the energy explained.

"You will fail," the D.M. screeched.

"Nope, this is *my* mind!" Zax screamed. "I will *not* fail!"

51

Zax woke up with Jack standing over him. "Oh, thank God. I thought you were dead," Jack said.

"What are we doing here?" Zax mumbled, noticing they were outside his old house. "How long have I been out?"

"About half an hour. I was afraid to leave you alone, and my phone has no signal here."

"Thanks for sticking around," Zax said, rising to his feet.

"No problem, "Jack said. "Just glad you're ok."

Suddenly, an intense tornado-like wind began funneling above the tree line. Zax looked up at the trees and again sensed an evil presence. It had to be the D.M. He grabbed his backpack off the ground and ran into the house. A few seconds later, he re-emerged in his suit, ready to take on the beast.

Jack froze; he instinctively knew that the monster must be near again.

No sooner than Zax exited the house, the D.M. came rushing from above. Zax shoved Jack out of the way and jumped back to dodge the D.M.

"You may have thrown me out of your mind, but I'm *still* stronger than you," the D.M. screeched.

"We'll see about that," Zax yelled fiercely.

The D.M. charged at Zax again, wings forcefully flapping. Zax managed to retrieve his scythe and slash the monster's wing before leaping out of its way. The D.M. wobbled past Zax, then recovered and flew back up for another attack.

Zax grabbed the blade of the scythe and threw it like a boomerang as the D.M. circled overhead. The beast dodged it, then turned and headed back for another round. This time, Zax took out his sword, slashed at the D.M., and as he expected, the D.M. caught it.

While the beast struggled with the sword, Zax created a new scythe behind his back and prepared for a swing at its neck. He knew if he missed, he would be vulnerable, and the beast would likely kill him.

Zax focused all his energy as he made one last powerful swing. The D.M. was caught off guard, and the scythe slashed across its neck, cutting off its head. As the head fell to the ground, the D.M. evaporated like the other beasts, but this time, a sheet of paper was among the purple dust.

Zax ran over and snatched up the cryptic note. Written in red ink, it said:

"If you beat this creature like the other two, then come find me. I am at a castle on an uncharted island in the middle of the Pacific Ocean. Here are the coordinates. Come alone.

"I still don't know who you are, and you might make this difficult, but I *will* get you," Zax mumbled under his breath.

The Date

52

After his encounter with the beast, Zax immediately went home to check on Jenny and Ethan and tell them what happened. But when he got home and saw them having toast and coffee for dinner, he changed his mind. They were safe. Once he saw they were ok, he wasn't sure he needed to tell them anything other than he changed his mind about staying at Mark's. At least, for now.

"Hey. Um, where's dinner? I'm famished," he said at the absence of anything other than their toast.

"Well, since you were staying at Mark's, we decided not to cook and to just eat light," Jenny said. "By the way, what happened to staying at Mark's?"

"Just changed my mind and wanted to be home."

"Oh," Jenny said and decided not to pursue a more detailed explanation. "Want me to make you something?"

"No, it's ok. Don't want to be a bother," Zax said.

"It's no bother. I can make something if you're really hungry."

"No, I'm good. I'll just make myself a PB&J."

"You sure?"

"Yeah, I'm sure."

Zax took his sandwich up to his room and found it basically the same as he left it. The only thing different was the pile of folded laundry on his bed. "There's my phone!" he said, spotting it on his nightstand. A wave of relief flooded through him. That was, until he saw there were about fifty messages from Jaiden. The first few simply asked where he was and for him to call her. But as he continued to read, her messages got a little more aggressive. He had no idea that she had that kind of vocabulary.

Zax took the last bite of his PB&J and picked up his phone to call her. Just as he reached to punch in her number, it started to ring. It was Jaiden. He debated whether or not to answer because he thought he might lose his hearing if he did. He'd heard her yell before, and he fully expected to be blasted if he picked up. But then he decided he didn't care. He needed to talk to her.

On the third ring, he answered, "Hello."

"Zax?" she said softly. It sounded as if she had been crying. This was certainly not the response he had anticipated.

"Hey, are you ok?" he asked.

"No! You haven't been responding to my text or calls. Why didn't you tell me about this D.M. thing?" she asked, sniffling.

"I didn't want you to get hurt, or worse..." he said. "How did you even find out?"

"You shouldn't worry about me. I got Mark to talk, and he told me everything."

"But I *have* to worry about you. I have to worry about everyone. I was given this power to worry."

"You should have someone by your side," she said.

Zax sat for a moment without responding and thought about what she said. She was right. He *did* need someone by his side. This was the perfect opportunity to do something he'd wanted to do for a long time. It was time, and he decided he was going to do it. He was going to ask her out. Besides, he thought, this might get her off the topic of why he hadn't been in touch.

"Jaiden?" he said nervously.

"Yeah?"

Zax closed his eyes and took a deep breath. "Do you want to go on a date with me?" There was a long pause. Even though he couldn't see her, he envisioned an image of Jaiden's surprised face.

"Yes!" she said quietly, then repeated "yes" louder a few more times. "I've been hoping you would ask!"

"You have?" he asked, surprised.

"Yes. Is that bad?"

"No, just unexpected. Anyplace you'd like to go?" Zax asked, barely able to think.

"Hmmm. How about your old house? A lakeside picnic would be romantic," she said.

He grinned and tried to remain cool. "Ok. Sounds great. How about tomorrow afternoon? I get off work at one o'clock, so how about two-thirty?"

"Sounds amazing," she said.

"Ok. See you then?"

"See you then. Bye," Jaiden said and hung up the phone.

He'd done it. He had finally asked her out. Zax laid the phone back on his nightstand, fell backwards on to his bed, and yelled loudly, "YES!"

A few seconds later, Jenny and Ethen barged in.

"What happened?" Ethan asked as he forcefully flung open Zax's door.

"We heard you yell," Jenny said. "Is everything alright?"

"Everything's fine," Zax said, smiling. "I just asked Jaiden out on a date."

"What? That's fantastic!" Jenny said excitedly.

"That takes a lot of bravery and guts," Ethan said.

"So, where are you going?" Jenny asked.

"Why? So you can follow me and spy on us? Ha. I don't think so," Zax chuckled.

"You do remember that we have a scanner that can find you no matter where you go, right?" Ethan joked.

"You wouldn't do that. That would be a new low even for you," Zax said.

"Watch us," Jenny replied with the creepiest face he'd ever seen. Then she laughed.

"Fine. We're going back to the old house to have a picnic on the lake tomorrow afternoon."

"That will be a really nice place for a date," Jenny said. "The house is still a mess, but it's a beautiful spot."

"Yep. Jaiden picked it out."

"Good idea." Ethan winked at Zax. "Figure out where *she* thinks would be a good place."

"So...you won't try to follow me since I told you?"

"No, we won't follow you. We promise," Ethan assured him.

"Ok, good," Zax said and hoped he meant it.

Jenny gave Zax a hug, and she and Ethan left his room. He went to bed right away. He wanted to be well-rested for his date tomorrow.

53

Zax woke up, ate, took a shower, and got ready for work. He'd been thinking about the note left by the creature all night and decided he needed to tell Ethan and Jenny. At some point, he would have to find the castle in the Pacific and knew he needed help pinpointing the exact position. Ethan looked at the note and said he would request the office's locating team define the location of the coordinates as soon as possible.

Zax got to work and was pleasantly surprised to enter the building without bullets flying at him. *Finally*, he thought. The morning passed with him doing stuff like making copies, sorting papers, and things like that. Perfectly non-stressful.

But it didn't last. As he was reading over a document about the history of the agency, bullets began to whiz by him—he was totally blindsided. He scrambled under the table and created a shield. He could not believe he allowed himself to think they were going to let a shift pass without shooting at him. *Really?* he thought. Once again, he had to protect himself from his co-workers.

When he got home from work, he grabbed the picnic basket that Jenny had prepared for his date and took off. As he neared the old house, Jaiden was sitting by the lake.

"You weren't waiting long, were you?" Zax asked as he got closer.

"No, I just got here. Hope the blanket is ok. I thought we could use something to sit on."

"It's perfect," he grinned. He sat down and placed the basket between them. "So, have you ever been on a date before?"

Her eyes widened. She tensed up. "Yeah, how about you?"

"No. This is my first," Zax said and took the ham and cheese sandwiches out of the basket. *Now what?* he wondered. *Just eat? I don't know how to go on a date. She seemed nervous earlier. Maybe this was a mistake.*

"Hey, if you don't want to do this, we don't have to," Zax said and started to get up.

Jaiden grabbed his sleeve and pulled him back down. "Of course, I want to do this," she said. "As soon as I sat next to you during lunch that first day, I wanted to do this. You're the exact opposite of all those bullies. You're caring, nice, and I could tell you would stand up for the little guy. But I was just afraid of being hurt again."

There was another awkward silence before she added, "How about we eat that picnic you brought? I'm starving!"

"Me too," Zax smiled. He placed their sandwiches on a napkin and pulled out some chips. "If you don't mind me asking, what do you mean by 'again'?"

"I should probably tell you," she sighed. "At my other school, I had a boyfriend. He was more like Jack used to be—a football quarterback who bullied other kids. I didn't like it, so I tried asking him to stop. When I did, he slapped me to the ground and walked away. After that, it just became worse. His bullying intensified, and every time he saw me, he aggressively grabbed my arm and threw me around. One time it was really bad. He ended up ripping my shirt. He laughed and took a picture, then posted it all over school. It even got around to the teachers and parents. Nowhere was safe," she explained quietly. "That's the real reason we moved here."

Zax was furious. No, what he was, couldn't be described with words. His energy started to boil up, overflow, and seep from his body. Though he tried to contain it, Jaiden could see his anger.

"There's no need to be mad," she said. "I heard he got arrested a while ago for that and a lot of other stuff."

Zax couldn't help it. His anger was overflowing, and no one could calm him down. The energy was building up, getting bigger and bigger, and swirling all around him. He yelled with an intensity unlike anything before. All the energy went hurling through the air with a massive explosion. Trees toppled throughout the forest, and the water in the lake was forced away from them. Behind them, windows were blown out of Zax's old house. Jaiden's long blond hair was going crazy, going all over the place, all over her head. For a second, he felt like his strength, speed, reflexes, etc., had all multiplied 100-fold. Then, in a flash, the energy was gone. Everything was completely still.

Zax took a deep breath. *What just happened?* he thought. He looked at Jaiden. She was lying on her back with her eyes wide open, staring at him.

"What was *that*?" Jaiden asked calmly, afraid to move.

"I'm not sure," he said, looking down at his hands. "It's not the first time something like this has happened. I'm sorry if I scared you. This same thing happened during my training while we were on our field trip."

"Well, that certainly wasn't like the other times. This was *so* much stronger."

She paused and turned her attention to the sky. "Maybe your anger made it more powerful. Or maybe it was just something entirely different."

This energy *was* different, but Zax didn't know why. He wondered if it had to do with his training. *No. That couldn't be it. Maybe a part of it, but it couldn't have just been just the training alone. It must have been something else,* he thought.

All of a sudden, cars from the office surrounded them, and agents popped out with guns drawn. Zax tried bringing up the energy to protect them, but he couldn't. He'd depleted the energy like he had when they were on the field trip. He started to get dizzy and couldn't walk. He fell over and passed out. Once again, he was in the dark room with a very dim light.

"I ran out of energy, again, didn't I?" he asked.

"Yes," the energy said.

"What just happened?" Zax asked.

"I don't know," it said.

"How do you *not* know?" Zax quizzed, discouraged. "You're the one who's had all the answers so far."

"I don't know, but it has to do with your emotion, that's for sure. Your rage that someone hurt Jaiden," it said.

"That makes…" Zax let his words trail off.

"But if you can learn how to fully control this stronger energy, you'll be unstoppable."

"First, I need to get my energy back."

"Yes, you do."

"How do I do that?"

"The same as before. But maybe you shouldn't jump out of a plane this time. By now, the office has probably made something to help."

"Ok, so how do I leave from this dream or whatever this place is?"

"I don't know how," the energy replied. "But I know you're going to leave right now."

"Wait. What?"

54

Zax woke up in a hospital bed at the office with Jenny and Ethan at his side.

"What happen?" he asked, trying to focus.

"You passed out of exhaustion," Jenny said.

"Is Jaiden ok?" Zax asked.

"Yes, but she's very worried about you," Jenny answered.

"I guess I ran out of energy, literally."

"Concerning that, we have some good news. We have developed a machine that we think will replenish your energy. You won't have to jump out of an airplane in a lightning storm over and over," Ethan said.

"Great. Because as you know, it's quite a distance to the middle of the Pacific, and I'm going to need maximum energy once I get there," Zax said as he sat up in bed, thinking about the note left from the third beast. "Wait. How do you know about me being able to run out of energy?"

"Don't worry about that right now. We need to get you recharged," Jenny said. "Do you feel strong enough to walk?"

"Yeah, I do. Let's go."

Jenny and Ethan led Zax into a huge pentagon-shaped room filled with giant Tesla coils in each corner.

"What is this room?" Zax asked.

"After it became clear that your energy could be temporarily depleted and then recharged by lightning—which we now know is just condensed energy—the office converted an old energy experiment into this state-of-the-art charging station tailored specifically for you. The energy is captured from lightning and stored in giant batteries. You will need to position yourself in the center of the room," Ethan explained before he and Jenny proceeded into the adjacent room.

"Wait a minute, is this thing safe?" Zax asked.

"Theoretically, yes, but we haven't had anyone to test in on," Jenny said. "The director and several technicians will be watching by way of cameras and will shut down the device if anything goes wrong. You ready?"

"Whenever you are," Zax replied with a thumb's up.

"Ok, we're starting now," Ethan said.

The oversized coils started up with a mild humming noise and bright yellow glow. They got louder and louder and brighter and brighter. A stream of energy then arced from the top of one of the coils to Zax's body, followed very closely by streams from the second, third, fourth, and fifth coils. The light created by the energy streams seemed to dance rhythmically around the room. Then a giant burst of energy flowed into Zax's body. From the look on his face, Jenny and Ethan thought it must have hurt like hell. After a few seconds, Zax's painful look was replaced by a smile. The energy began to feel warm and soothing to him. Quickly, he went from feeling slow and sluggish to feeling as though he could run a marathon. After about a minute, the noise and energy flow stopped as the coils were shut down.

"That's enough for today," a voice said over the intercom. We gave you a low-level dose for 60 seconds, and it looks like you tolerated it well."

The Mastery

55

After the recharging operation was finished, Zax told Jenny and Ethan about the giant burst of energy that was directed into his body and how it was stronger and different than the lightning strikes. He believed he was able to store a greater quantity of this energy. He also explained that through practice, he might be able to retain the increased quantities for longer periods of time. If this were the case, he felt he would be virtually unstoppable.

"How are you sure that this is so different from the rest of the energy you use?" Ethan asked.

"I don't know, to be honest. But as it started building up, I felt stronger, like all my skill levels had gone through the roof for a short period of time," Zax explained.

56

Training resumed the next weekend. Zax seriously regretted telling Ethan and Jenny about the new energy because they intensified his training to the nth degree. It was as if they were preparing him to run around the world in five minutes. His activities now included physical training, five sessions a day of the hardest hologram level, five shooting sessions with the targets so far away he could barely see them, and a new challenge, the recharge room. Using the recharge room consisted of two steps. First, he practiced using bursts of energy in the same way he did at the lake until his energy was almost depleted. Then he entered the recharge room, where his energy level was restored. Technicians varied the time, amount, and rate that the energy flowed into his body to test his energy management capabilities. This was also done five times a day.

"Is all this necessary?" Zax asked, mentally exhausted after his final session of the day a couple of weeks later.

"Of course," Jenny said.

"You're the one that said you needed the additional energy capacity and the skills to control it," Ethan added.

"Yes, but I can do all the holograms at the hardest level perfectly and hit every bullseye at the farthest target."

"Maybe. But you couldn't control even a quarter of the energy you had when you were on your date. The director thinks you still need more practice and experience," Ethan said.

"Then why not focus on that one thing. Why am I wasting time on the other stuff?"

"Because you need to stay sharp in all departments, physically and mentally," Jenny answered.

"I think I'm sharp enough."

"You can be ten times sharper. You said when you had your burst, everything got stronger, so we need to work on everything," Ethan said.

"I guess you're right," Zax sighed. As he reached for his bottled water, his phone dinged with a text from Jaiden asking if they could meet up behind school. Over the past few weeks, he'd been spending all his free time with her and hoped that sooner or later, one of them would have the courage to say that they were officially dating.

"Need to go," he said, smiling at his phone.

"Ok. See you later," Jenny said to his back. By the look on his face, there was no doubt in her mind that the text came from Jaiden.

Zax got to school and saw her waiting next to the largest tree on campus. *How does she always get here before me? Am I really that slow?* he wondered.

"Hey, I hope you weren't waiting long," he said as he approached.

"No, I wasn't," Jaiden said.

"Ok, good. So, what did you want to talk about?"

"I've been thinking about this a lot since our date, and I decided…" she said, looking down, not finishing her sentence.

Zax's heart raced. He didn't know what to think other than she was about to say she didn't want to be friends. He didn't say anything. But then, to his surprise, she walked over and kissed him and whispered, "I love you," in his ear.

His face turned bright red, and he felt like he was about to collapse. It was his first kiss.

Zax began to feel the energy surround him in the same manner it did when he was in the forest, getting stronger and stronger. But the energy in the forest was everywhere and frantic. Now it was more like an aura coming off his body.

"I think I'm starting to get the hang of this," Zax smiled.

"Hang of what?"

"This skill that will make me unstoppable. I think it has to do with emotion."

"I guess that makes sense. With the anger in the forest and now love…it does seem to make sense. You were able to control this emotion much better than you were with the anger," she encouraged.

"Yeah, I was," he said, staring into her eyes.

The moment was perfect until it wasn't. Zax's phone vibrated in his pocket, and though he didn't want to answer, he knew he had to. It was Jenny.

"Hey," he answered. "What's going on?"

"We just got a major energy spike from you at the office." Zax could hear the panicked tone in her voice.

"Oh it was nothing. Just practicing," he said, looking at Jaiden.

"You should do that here; someone might see you. Dinner is about ready, so come home soon."

"Ok, I'll be there shortly."

Zax put his phone away and reached out to grab Jaiden's hand. "I'm sorry, but I have to go. That was Jenny, and she said I needed to be home soon."

They continued to talk for a few minutes, then he leaned over and kissed her cheek. "See you tomorrow?" he asked, wishing he could stay.

"Yeah," she said. "See you tomorrow."

He had no idea where his confidence had come from, but wherever it came from, he hoped it stayed. Jaiden's words lingered with him. He wondered if he should've told her he loved her too.

57

The following day, Zax's training continued in full force—the workouts, the holograms, the gun range, the resistance, and the recharging. As the days passed, he spent as much time as he could with Jaiden, but training came first. Even on the days he could not see her, he talked to her during the few breaks that Ethan and Jenny allowed him to have.

While he was training, he was constantly monitored by office personnel to assure that he was maintaining control and utilizing the energy safely. He believed that some of the agents were beginning to build confidence in his abilities—and quite possibly even like him. Things were great. But storm clouds loomed in the distance.

One morning a few weeks later, Jaiden suddenly went quiet and stopped responding to his calls or texts. He began to worry that he'd upset her somehow or, worse, that something had happened to her.

"Zax, come here. You've got to see this," Jenny yelled from the living room late that evening. "Hurry."

Zax sprinted into the room and saw Jenny standing in front of the TV.

"Yeah, what's up? Did you hear from Jaiden?" he asked.

Jenny stepped aside and pointed to the television. "Jaiden has been kidnapped!" Jenny exclaimed. "And the kidnapper has written a letter addressed to you!" She paused the news broadcast on the note shown on the screen.

"Zax, I have your girlfriend. She will make a great subject for my next experiment. This is what you get for snooping around other people's computers. You know how to find me. I told you after you killed my third creature. The clock is ticking."

Zax could feel rage ripping through him. Now he knew. There was only one person the kidnapper could be. And it was the same person who created the three beasts. It could only be…Professor Brian.

Zax immediately headed to the office where he blasted into the recharge room. He set the dial for the highest energy recharge level for a full five minutes. When the cycle was completed, he was charged with more than double the amount of the energy that he released in the blast at the lake.

"PROFESSOR BRIAN!" he screamed. "I'M COMING FOR YOU!"

The Castle

58

Zax rushed out of the recharge room and into the communications center. He needed to find out exactly where this island was. To his surprise, a group of agents was standing in front of a large computer screen. The screen displayed a detailed map they had generated from the coordinates showing the location of the island.

"Move out of my way," Zax shouted as he shoved his way through the group before being blocked by a short, stocky man he'd never seen before.

"I'm the son of the man that runs this place. My name is Walter Moore. We were told not to let you have this map," he said, staring up at Zax. "Some of the people here feel like your motive in trying to rescue Jaiden is good, and they would do the same thing to save their loved ones. But others are afraid you will lose control because of your emotions. If you lose control, they're concerned that many innocent lives will be lost, and property will be destroyed. However, everybody knows that even if we all took you on at once, we wouldn't be able to stop you."

"And where do you stand?" Zax asked, staring into Walter's eyes.

"Both," he said and pulled out a pistol. Upon seeing Walter pull his weapon, everyone in the room followed suit. "I think you're the only one who can save that girl, but you could lose control. So, prove to me that you know what you're doing."

Zax thought for a moment. "Who is with me?" he asked.

Half the agents walked around and stood behind Zax, one handing him a gun as he passed by. The other half stood in front of the screen—the ones that wanted to stop him from going.

"You need to save your energy for the person who sent that letter," said one of the agents standing behind him.

"Thanks for giving me a chance," Zax said to those who stood with him. "But would everyone please stand down? I can take care of them," he said, nodding to the agents who were blocking the screen. "No one has to get hurt. I have more than enough energy to neutralize them and still save Jaiden and beat Professor Brian, that bastard."

Zax clenched his fist and glared at the agents blocking his path. He forged small pellets from his energy and used them to shoot the guns from their hands. He quickly transformed the pellets into a rope of energy and tied their wrists. "You should have known that you couldn't win," he said, scowling at their faces.

The agents standing in front of Zax stared at him in amazement and hurriedly moved out of his way. As he stepped through the parted crowd towards the screen, someone rushed in front of him and pointed a gun barrel right in his face. It was the director.

"I won't let you go; you could get lost in your feelings and destroy everything," Director Alvin said, standing in his way.

Zax put his forehead against the barrel. "You can kill me if you'd like, but only after I save Jaiden," he said and shoved the director's arm down. The director stumbled as Zax angrily bumped his shoulder and pushed him out of the way. He hit the print button, and immediately the map began printing on the adjacent printer. He ripped the paper off the printer and stormed towards the door.

"How do you know you won't lose control?" Director Alvin shouted to his back.

"Because Jaiden will be there to calm me down if I do," he yelled without turning around.

Walter followed Zax to the exit door. "Hey Zax," he called from behind.

Zax stopped and turned around.

"How are you going to get to the island?"

"I'll figure it out," Zax said.

"What about using one of our jets? We have a modified aircraft we think will meet your needs. It's currently programmed with the island's coordinates, is fueled up, and ready to go."

"Are you kidding me?" Zax asked, shocked at the offer. "Can the plane run on autopilot? I don't want anyone going except me."

"Why is that?" Walter asked.

"I don't want anyone else to get hurt or get in the way."

"I was kind of expecting that from you, to be honest," he said. "You're a good guy, Zax. And, yes, it can—and will be—remotely flown. You'll be going alone."

The small private jet was ready and waiting when Zax and Walter got to the airstrip outside the office. Zax had never flown on a private plane before. He'd only seen them in the movies where someone important was being transported. When he stepped inside, it was nicer than anything he had expected. It had large comfortable seats, lots of room to walk around, and a bar. But not a typical bar, this bar served frozen yogurt. He grinned. *How did they know? This is amazing!* he thought.

"You think I could have this plane?" Zax asked Walter jokingly.

"Ha," Walter laughed. "We've been secretly working on this for a few weeks. We converted it from a drone. It was specifically designed for you, complete with a frozen yogurt bar. It's yours to use on any mission. As for personal use…don't think so. It's our fastest transport medium. It will get you to the island faster than any of our other planes. It has sufficient fuel to circle the island for at least an hour and get you back here safely."

"Perfect," Zax said, taking a more serious tone. "It shouldn't take more than an hour. If all goes according to plan, I'll make an energy platform to transport us back up to the plane. But if I don't make it in time, bring the plane home."

"How will you and Jaiden get back if we do that?"

"I guess I'll just have to figure it out when I cross that bridge."

"If I can't keep my father away from the controls, there might be another problem," Walter said.

Zax knew Walter would do what he could. If it were left to Director Alvin, he would turn the jet back as soon as Zax got off and simply leave him there.

"That's alright. Do your best. I'll get Jaiden and myself back, one way or another," Zax stated.

"Good luck," Walter said, extending his hand. "There are parachutes on board just in case you need them." The two shook hands, and Walter stepped off the plane.

60

Zax buckled up, and within minutes, the jet was in the air. He was off to the small island that few people had ever seen—or heard of—prior to his battle with the D.M. He really hadn't needed the map of the island's location after all. The office, or at least Walter, was one step ahead of him.

Time passed slowly for Zax as the plane streaked through the cloudless sky. When the island finally came into sight, the path lighting on the jet's floor illuminated. The time had come. Zax unfastened his seatbelt and scrambled into his suit. Cautiously, he opened the exit door and looked out at the small island below, carefully studying its details. He took a deep breath and jumped into the unknown. "Here we go again…"

As Zax soared through the air on his descent towards the island, his mask came untied and flew off his face. He didn't care; it was the least of his concerns at the moment. Professor Brian and Jaiden knew it was him who wore the suit, so it was not a big deal. It was replaceable; Jaiden was not.

Getting closer to land, he was shocked at the enormity of what he saw below. A castle covered most of the island, and dense storm clouds hovered high above it. The entire scene reminded him of the evil layered castles portrayed in old black and white vampire movies. Not what he expected at all.

Zax began steering himself to a remote section of the castle roof. As he approached, he focused some of the energy into his feet and legs to help break his fall. After landing, he surrounded his hand with the energy, then punched a hole in the roof and dropped to the floor below. He landed in a room with tubes of chemicals and a rock that was oozing weird, yet familiar, stuff. The rock was in a glass case. The ooze was the same color as the beasts' dust when they evaporated—a weird purple color.

He stood for a moment scouring the room, then spotted an exit into a hallway. The hall was lined with gothic artwork and flaming torches on the walls. Someone had really succeeded in making this place seem like a medieval castle.

He crept down the hallway and found that it dead-ended into a large room that housed nothing but an oversized map of the island and a floorplan of the castle. Both were tacked to the back wall with daggers. The laboratory was clearly marked on the floorplan. It was apparent that Professor Brian wanted Zax to find him.

Zax studied the map and decided his best approach was to do a sneak attack on the Professor from the room above his lab. Once he memorized the map, he stealthily snuck through the castle to the room from which he would strike. Upon entering the room, he spotted a small crack in the floor big enough for him to see into the lab. Silently, he crept to the edge of the crack.

He could see and hear everything that was happening in the room below. Professor Brian was wearing a royal blue lab coat that struck him well below his knees, and Jaiden was inside a cage on the other side of the room.

"Why are you doing this?" Jaiden pleaded, shaking the cage.

"Zax destroyed my last chance of having a normal life!" Professor Brian yelled in his German accent. He sighed and crossed his arms. "Because he spied on my computer, I lost my teaching job and was sent back to prison. The thought of getting revenge was the only thing that kept me alive.

Then, out of nowhere, I was given an opportunity to escape and get revenge at the same time. But your relationship with Zax changed everything. Not only did he fall for you, but somehow you triggered the uncanny ability he possesses to protect himself from my creatures. You make him happy. And *nothing* will be more painful to him than losing you," he chuckled.

"How did you get the material to make these creatures? I've never seen anything like this stuff," Jaiden said, still trying to figure an escape.

"Oh, you're curious now?" he asked. "Fine. Since you won't be alive much longer in your current form, I'll tell you. Shortly after I was taken to prison, I was sitting alone in the courtyard when I heard a whooshing sound. I saw what looked like a rock the size of a tennis ball coming right at me from the sky. It crashed into the ground directly in front of me, and, amazingly enough, no one else noticed it. The rock was the darkest shade of black I had ever seen. I quickly hid it under my shirt. It was barely noticeable.

"To my surprise, I heard a deep mysterious voice coming from the rock which said, 'Hello, Brian. You were wronged. You were given a new life, and that kid, Zax, took it away from you. Now it's time for you to get your revenge. I have developed a goo that can turn living things into monsters that possess great powers. In this rock, there are three containers that are specified for certain living things—a lizard, a gorilla, and a bat. You will create, then release these beasts, one at a time, and they will inflict pain and ultimately kill Zax. All I ask in return is that you free me from my cell.'"

Professor Brian leaned against his lab table and continued. "I asked where the cell was, and it said, 'deep, deep in space, inside of a white hole.' Then it outlined what I would have to do to free it. I told the voice it had my word that I would do what it asked, but only after Zax was dead. The voice also told me about the boy's power and how it had been activated.

It was from your phone." He paused and snapped his fingers. "And just like that, the voice was gone.

"Snakes, lizards, and rodents are plentiful in and around a prison. Once I got my hands on a lizard, I created the first creature and used it to break out of that dastardly place. I stole money, food, and credit cards for survival and was forced into hiding. Later, I stole tracking equipment and placed a transmitter under the skin of the creature. It was given instructions to find and punish Zax and sent off in the direction of the school. When I noticed the creature had disappeared from the tracking radar, I knew that Zax had defeated it. With the authorities breathing down my neck and one of my creatures dead, I knew I had to find a better hiding place. A relative of mine, who owes me a favor, owns this island and is allowing me to hide out and experiment here. Virtually no one knows about the island, and the authorities will never be able to find it. It's not on any map, so it turned out to be the perfect place to create and send the other two creatures from."

"And you're not questioning what this mysterious voice is that's stuck in a white hole? *Are you crazy?* And what the heck is a 'white hole' anyway?" Jaiden asked.

"Details, details. As long as I can get my revenge, I would sell my soul to the devil. Now, I want to test what would happen if I put all three of these specific oozes into one living creature. Science believes that humans evolved from creatures like gorillas, maybe even fish. A lizard is close enough, and who knows about bats. So, if all three would be compatible with anything, I believe it would be humans. You, my dear, will make the perfect test subject for my theory," Professor Brian said, clearly stating his diabolical intent.

Zax heard everything. He knew he was just in time. He had to do something before the Professor got to Jaiden. As Professor Brian reached for the vials of purple ooze, Zax crashed through the ceiling and hurtled into the room. Jaiden was still trapped in the cage.

"I won't let you touch her," Zax yelled as he hit the floor.

"Ahhh…you finally got here," Professor Brian said with a demented smile.

"Let Jaiden go!" Zax demanded.

"And why would I do that?"

"Because you want me. She has nothing to do with this."

"Oh, but she does. She has everything to do with this."

"Oh yeah, how?"

"She is the one who started all of this by giving you her phone. When it touched your hand, your power started to emerge. Later you used that power on me. Remember detention when I caught you looking at my computer? Because of her phone unleashing your powers, I ended up going to jail. She is also the one person who makes you happy. Quite possibly, you're in love. So, as you can see, she is not only a part of it, she's *the key* to it."

Professor Brian paused and glanced over Zax's shoulder at Jaiden. "Plus, I need to test this on someone," he said, looking at Jaiden with an evil grin.

"Then do it on yourself," Zax yelled.

"And become one of those mindless beasts? I don't think so," Professor Brian laughed.

Zax looked over at Jaiden and thought of all the pain and destruction he had caused her. He'd destroyed her phone, left her with a knife-wielding maniac, snuck into her house because he had nowhere else to go, and made her worry at the beach when he fought the Brute. And now, because of him, she was in a cage.

Jaiden saw distress and sorrow on his face. "It's not your fault, Zax. I *decided* to stay with you. If I hadn't wanted to, I would've stayed away from the beginning, but I didn't. I *want to be* with you," she said.

Zax looked at her with wide eyes that were starting to tear up.

"Stop it with this love bull crap," Professor Brian snapped as he began to push buttons on his lab table.

A hatch under Jaiden's cage slowly opened and exposed a vat filled with ooze. The cage jolted and began to lower into the vat.

"Being a brilliant genius, I was able to reverse engineer the ooze," Professor Brian gloated. "This vat is full of it!"

Zax was angrier than he'd ever been, and a heaviness was building in his chest, but oddly, it was a nice feeling. The only thing he could think of at this moment was trying to protect Jaiden from all harm. That feeling had to be from his love for her.

The energy was building up more and more, even more than it had in the woods. Zax yelled as loud as he possibly could, but instead of exploding out, the energy surrounded him like it did when Jaiden kissed him. Everything from his speed to his strength increased a thousand-fold. Zax ran to the cage, and with his enhanced strength, he split the cage in half. The energy around him dissipated. He helped Jaiden out of the cage, and they started to walk out of the room. Professor Brian jumped in front of them.

"You're not going anywhere! Do you think you can just walk out of here?" he screamed.

"Move! You've lost! You will never win!" Zax blasted.

"We'll see about that!" Professor Brian ran over to the counter and grabbed the three vials of ooze labeled "Lizard," "Gorilla," and "Bat."

These must have been the Chupacabra, the Brute, and the D.M., Zax thought as he read the labels from across the room.

"I think I will take your advice and test these on myself," Professor Brian yelled.

As Zax and Jaiden watched, he emptied all three oozes into one syringe and injected the contents into his arm. Slowly, his face contorted. He started to scream and fell to the ground. It seemed that the mixture was more than he could take. *Just what he deserves!* Zax thought.

Zax grabbed Jaiden's arm and continued walking towards the door when suddenly, he heard a soft humming sound coming from Professor Brian's body. He turned around to find Professor Brian growing larger and larger. His skin was turning into the scales of the Chupacabra, his head into that of a dragon, his legs into those of a lizard, and his body was taking the form of a snake. The scales were red like the Brute. Through the scales grew the wings of the D.M. The only resemblance to Professor Brian was that this beast still had his disheveled white hair on top of its dragon head.

"What the hell!" Zax mumbled.

"Now we'll see who wins," the creature said in a new, distorted, screechy voice. This was no longer Professor Brian. This was now a dangerous, evil mutation bent on revenge and carnage.

Zax nudged Jaiden towards the door. "Jaiden, run! Keep going until you find an exit. I'll catch up with you."

"But won't you need help with this thing? He looks *extremely* powerful," Jaiden cried, out of fear for Zax.

"I'll be ok as long as I know you're safe," he said frantically. "Now go!"

"You'd better come back to me in one piece," she said, running out the door.

"No one is leaving here!" the creature screamed and rushed toward her.

Zax created a spear and threw it at the creature, but he used his powerful wings to fly up and dodge it.

"You won't hurt anyone as long as I'm here," Zax proclaimed.

Jaiden made it out of the room before the creature could reach her. It then swung around in Zax's direction, knocking over equipment and spilling chemicals. By that time, Zax had recovered the spear and was ready for battle.

He aimed the spear to hit the creature between the eyes like he did with the Chupacabra, but the creature dodged again. He created and threw a second spear—the one with the tether connected to his wrist—into the ceiling and yanked himself up above the creature. He pulled his sword and tried slashing what use to be the Professor's arm, but the sword bounced off its scales. He then traded the sword for his scythe and tried to slash the creature's wing. But there were also scales on the wings.

This beast shouldn't be able to fly! Zax thought. *The scales should prevent him from flying. How does he do that?*

Zax had one last resort. The question was, did he have enough energy. There was one only way to find out.

He started to concentrate on storing up more and more energy. He then let out a thunderous yell and was thrust into the energy aura state again. He leaped into the air, and for the first time, he realized that he could fly. He accomplished this by pushing a continuous stream of energy off the bottom of his feet, similar to the way a jet engine works. He wondered why he hadn't tried this before. With the discovery of yet another new skill, he became more confident that he could defeat this monster.

He paused for a moment, then flew directly at the creature. He passed by it in a flash and suddenly realized that he was on the other side of the room. He spun around quickly not wanting to let the creature get the upper hand. Then he saw it. The creature had a gaping hole in its chest; Zax had flown completely through its body.

But the hole seemed to have no impact. It began to disappear. The creature was still in attack mode. Instantly, Zax began to have an odd feeling that everything had changed. Even the weapons.

He pulled out the spear. It was now three times bigger and had a blade on both sides. His sword was now a two-handed broad sword. His scythe had changed into a type of quad scythe with a round wheel-like center. An energy rod extended out from each quadrant of the center handle, and a scythe blade was attached to the end of each energy rod. With the deluxe spear, the two-handled broad sword, and quad scythe, it was only a matter of time before he secured victory.

Zax threw the spear, and it went straight through the creature as fast as lightning, as if it had no scales. The creature shuddered. He pulled out his sword and swiped at it, cutting off one of its wings. This time, the creature screamed and lunged towards Zax. Cabinets crashed to the floor. The Professor's computer went flying into a wall.

Zax forced the four arms of the scythe weapon to begin spinning around the handle, making it act like a saw blade, and whirled it at the creature. The scythe caught the creature off guard and cut off a bit of its tail and one of its legs. Again, the creature spun around, causing more damage to the lab.

Seeing how well that worked, Zax knew he had the solution. Using his new flying skill and the spinning scythe weapon, Zax flew up and cut another hole all the way through the creature's body. This time, he circled around and did this over and over until the creature looked like Swiss cheese and fell to the floor.

Zax thought it was dead, even though it did not evaporate like the other beasts. But then, something happened. The piece of the creature's tail, its leg, and its wing came flying back to its body, reconnecting from where they had been severed. All the holes Zax had made in its body started mending. Soon, it was as good as new.

"I am stronger than you will ever be!" the creature screeched angrily. "There is no hope for you or that girl!"

Zax had to think of something to stop the creature once and for all. A vision suddenly flashed through his mind, much like the vision he saw that first time he held Jaiden's phone. It was a vision of a star. He didn't understand until he took a more focused look. It was a weapon. It had a round handle like the quad scythe, but instead of the arms, it had a broad sword extending from it. On the ends, it had the head of the deluxe spear. It was huge.

When the vision was over, Zax took his energy and created the new weapon— the "broad deluxe quad star." The star worked like the quad scythe and spun around like a saw blade.

"You will pay for all the pain you have caused!" Zax yelled and threw the star at the creature with all the strength he had.

The star went rushing towards the midsection of the creature and sliced it in half in one pass. The two halves went tumbling apart. The star left a type of energy block where the wound was inflected. With this energy block in place, he hoped the creature could not become whole again.

"You will regret what you have done to me! Dax *will* destroy you!" the creature screamed. Then the two halves began to shake violently and started turning purple. The dragon head shrieked in pain. The two halves began shrinking and then evaporated into a pile of purple dust. The creature—Professor Brian, a.k.a. Professor Evil—was finally dead.

Dax? What did he mean by that? Zax wondered as he surveyed the carnage.

61

Zax ran out of the lab and found Jaiden in the hall right outside the door. He took her hand and led her out of the castle. The jet was nowhere in sight, just as he'd expected. Director Alvin had called it back.

Zax had used a considerable amount of his energy in the battle with the creature and, without the plane, he wasn't sure how he and Jaiden would get home.

Then an idea flashed in his head. If he could use his new flying skill to catch up with the jet before it got too far away, they might have a chance. But if his energy ran out before they reached the plane, he would black out and both would fall to their deaths in the icy waters of the Pacific. The big question was: Could he make it? He had to take the chance.

He looked into Jaiden's eyes. "There's only one way for us to get off this island. Do you trust me?" he asked.

"Always," Jaiden said and squeezed his hand tightly.

He created an energy connection between them and said, "Ok. Here we go."

Zax again went into his energy aura mode and flew the two of them up and away from the island. He flew as fast as he could, following the same path the jet had taken to fly him there. He and Jaiden had been in the air about fifteen minutes when he caught a faint glimpse of the jet. He was starting to feel weak, but he knew he had to reach the plane.

He took a deep breath, and with a giant boost, he shot them over halfway to the jet. They got closer and closer, but he was quickly running out of energy.

With one final push, he caught up with the speeding jet and used a small amount of his remaining energy to hold on to the right wing. He made his way up the wing to an exterior button that opened an automatic door and pressed it. The door opened, and, using his last bit of strength, he slowly drug himself and Jaiden inside. He fell straight to the floor and passed out.

62

When Zax woke up, he was back in the hospital bed at the office. Jaiden was by his side, and Jenny and Ethan were just walking in.

"I've got to stop waking up here," he mumbled.

"You're ok!" Jaiden exclaimed, relieved.

"Of course I'm ok. Who do you think I am?" Zax smiled and reached for her hand.

"What happened?" Ethan asked, standing at the foot of Zax's hospital bed.

Zax told him and Jenny everything that happened. They looked at each other then back at him.

"Dax? What's that?" Ethan asked.

"I have no idea, but I don't think it's anything good."

"What makes you say that? How do you know?" Jenny asked.

"I don't know. It sounds familiar, but I'm not sure why. It's really foggy, but for some reason, I just don't have a good feeling about it."

"Why don't you try and rest for now," Jenny said. "We'll be back to check on you later." She bent down and kissed Zax on his forehead. "See you soon," she whispered in his ear.

As soon as Ethan and Jenny left the room, Zax turned his attention back to Jaiden. "So, did you mean what you said at the castle?" Zax asked.

"About being with you? Of course I meant it. If I thought being with you was going to be too much trouble, I would've stayed away from the beginning," she said.

Still holding his hand, Jaiden leaned over and kissed him. "Now that you're awake, I'm going to step out and call Jack and Mark and let them know you're ok. I know they want to see you too."

He watched as she walked towards the door. When the door closed behind her, he whispered to himself, "I don't know who or what Dax is, but if it's something bad, I won't let it hurt anyone. *Especially* Jaiden."

The saga continues…

A new novel by Dennis Eaves

Coming Soon

About the Author

Dennis Cazie Eaves is a senior at Summit High School in Mansfield, Texas. He enjoys reading fantasy, watching sci-fi, some anime, and all things gaming. In addition to being a talented writer, he is also a gifted artist—both traditional and digital.

Dennis is currently working on his second novel and looking forward to beginning college in 2021. To learn more about Dennis, check out his author page at leastreetpress.com. You may contact Dennis directly at authorzax@gmail.com.

www.ingramcontent.com/pod-product-compliance
Lightning Source LLC
Chambersburg PA
CBHW022357110726

47902CB00002BA/327